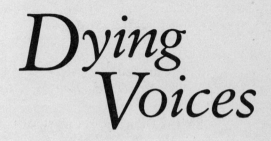

By Bill Crider

Carl Burns mystery
One Dead Dean

Sheriff Dan Rhodes mysteries
Death on the Move
Cursed to Death
Shotgun Saturday Night
Too Late to Die

Dying Voices

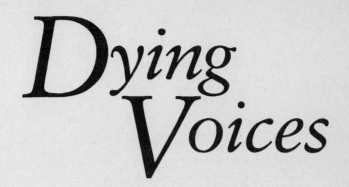

• Bill Crider •

St. Martin's Press ● New York

Design by *Amelia Mayone*

Library of Congress Cataloging-in-Publication Data
Crider, Bill.
  Dying voices.
    p. cm.
  "A Thomas Dunne book."
  ISBN 0-312-03328-1
  I. Title.
PS3553.R497D9 1989   813'.54—dc20 89-34853

First Edition

10 9 8 7 6 5 4 3 2 1

To Ruth Cavin

the editor every mystery writer
should be lucky enough to find

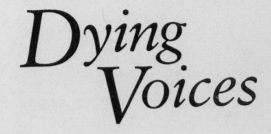

Dying Voices

·1·

Sometime over the summer, the pigeons had come back.

Carl Burns sat at his desk waiting for class to begin on the first day of the fall semester, and he could hear them in the attic above his head, doing whatever it was that they did up there. It sounded to him as if they were scurrying around on the rafters, running up and down them, and he could almost hear the sound their little toes, or claws, or talons, or whatever the hell it was that birds had, made on the wood as they raced around madly in the musty dark.

Now and then there would be a sudden flurry of wings as one of them took to the air, and because it was very dark up there, the fluttering might be followed by the soft sound they made when one of them collided with the beams that held up the roof.

When that happened, at least if the bird hit hard enough to addle its inconsiderable brain, it would plummet down to the acoustical tile in the false ceiling and land with a thud that dislodged a sizable amount of dirt and dust, not to mention an occasional dab of what Burns was certain must be pigeon shit, though he would never have admitted that to Mal Tomlin, who often insisted that Burns would one day be buried under tons of that very material when the ceiling collapsed from its accumulated weight.

Actually, there weren't tons of it up there, as Burns had discovered more or less by accident the previous fall, but there was enough to make things unpleasant, and some of it would come drifting down every time a pigeon fell. Everything about the situation contributed to a distinctly unpleasant odor on the third floor of Main.

In fact—

"It smells like you've got plumbing problems, kid." Mal Tomlin came through the door, smoking a Merit Menthol 100. "Here, take one of these. It'll cut the stink a little bit."

He reached into his shirt pocket and pulled out a crumpled pack, tapped out a cigarette, and flipped it to Burns, who fumbled it and bent it a bit. He straightened it carefully and tossed it back.

"I quit again over the summer," Burns said.

Tomlin put the cigarette carefully back in the pack and inserted the pack in his pocket. Then he took a thoughtful drag on the Merit. "I give you two days," he said.

"Two days for what?"

"Two days before you either die of the smell or you start smoking in self-defense. What the hell *is* that, anyway?" He eased his compact form into the chair that students used when they came in for conferences about their papers and started looking around for an ashtray.

There wasn't one. Burns had made sure of that, to put temptation out of his way. However, Burns had just finished drinking his breakfast Mr. Pibb, so he fished the can out of the trash and gave it to Tomlin.

"You of all people should know what that smell is," Burns said after Tomlin had carefully tapped ashes through the opening in the can.

"Me?" Tomlin ran one hand through his thinning ginger-colored hair. He appeared genuinely puzzled. "Is that

· 2 ·

some kind of a crack, right here on the first day of the semester?"

"It's no crack. Listen."

They sat there in silence. From the attic came the sounds of scurrying, fluttering, and now, cooing.

"Oh my God," Tomlin said. "Pigeons."

"That would be my guess, all right," Burns said.

"Who knows what kind of disease the little bastards are carrying," Tomlin said, "Polio, probably, or something like that. What's that stuff you get from parrots in Mexico? Shit-a-cosis?" Tomlin was chairman of the Education Department, but big words were not his specialty.

"Psittacosis," Burns told him. "It's some kind of virus, I think."

"Well, I bet you get it from shit, then," Tomlin said. "The dry stuff's one thing. It's been up there forever. But with those new birds flying around and stirring things up, you never can tell what might happen. And naturally all the new stuff, wet and nasty like it is, will just add to the problem." He gave a significant glance upward at the already darkly stained acoustical tile above them.

As if to justify that gloomy forecast, two of the birds apparently got into some kind of territorial dispute in the darkness. There were a couple of loud calls and a great deal of wing beating. One of them flew into a beam and came crashing down right overhead.

Dirt rained down on Burns's desk, followed by a lone feather that wafted gently after.

"Shit-a-cosis!" Tomlin yelped, scrambling to his feet, and getting as far from the desk as he could. He dropped his cigarette into the soft drink can and fled. "I'll talk to you later, maybe," he called as he passed through the door. "But not here!"

Burns had not seen Tomlin much over the summer, but he was not sad about his leaving. There were a few things Burns still had to do before class got started, including finding copies of his course syllabus and his list of rules and regulations relating to attendance and tardiness. He had typed them and had them duplicated the previous spring, and he found them in the filing cabinet after taking time to brush off his desk.

The administration at Hartley Gorman College was fond of informing the faculty members that they were to keep the students in class for the full time at all meetings, including the first one, not an easy task when the students had not bought a textbook, much less read anything in it. Still, Burns felt the obligation, thanks to numerous reminders, that "The students are paying for credit hours."

What he liked to do was spend the time explaining the rules and telling the students what they could expect. Since his first class was a sophomore survey of American literature, they could expect a lot of reading, beginning with the Puritans (though Burns got over that section of the book pretty quickly) and finishing with a few contemporary writers (another section that Burns tended to give short shrift). They could also expect a term paper of about ten pages, two major essay quizzes (mid-semester and final) and daily quizzes on the reading. Anyone missing class fifteen times would be dropped with an *F* and there would be no make-ups on the daily quizzes.

That was all there was to it, and Burns was hard pressed to stretch it to fifty minutes. Sometimes he was able to go for forty-five, though. He was glad it wasn't a Tuesday/Thursday class.

Once he had his materials in hand, he was ready to go, but there were still thirty minutes until class. Burns always got to school at least an hour before classes began, which on Mondays, Wednesdays, and Fridays, meant that he arrived at seven A.M.

He decided to devote the extra time to working on his list of the things that could go wrong the next weekend.

The list and the Pilot Razor Point pen he liked to write with were in the thin drawer in the middle of his desk. While he was rummaging around looking for it, he found a list from last year, one he had never completed, listing the things he hated most. High on the list were the words "Dean Elmore." After the dean's untimely demise—untimely in that it had not occurred several years earlier, Burns thought—the list had lain uncompleted. Burns had never had the heart to go back to it.

He looked at it briefly, then crossed off Elmore's name. He didn't hate the man any more, though he had to admit that he did not have any fond memories of him.

He tossed the paper back into the drawer and found the piece he was looking for. It was headed "Things that Can Go Wrong with the Edward Street Seminar." It was a list that had haunted him for most of the summer, and he had begun compiling it only one day after HGC's new president had called him in near the end of the spring semester.

Franklin Miller, the new president, was a fairly young man for the job, not more than forty, Burns thought. He had little experience in college administration, but a great deal of expertise in raising money. As such, he was ideal for HGC, a school that needed money at least as much as it needed leadership.

The former president had been possessed of little talent in either area, and because of other flaws in his character, discovered mainly by Burns, he was now residing in an expensive psychiatric facility, which really wasn't bad considering that the other option was a much less comfortable residence in the Texas Department of Corrections.

Miller was a wonderful representative of the school. He had a firm handshake, a beautiful singing voice, which he used to advantage in the church choirs when he was on fundraising expeditions for the small denominational school, a number of dark blue suits and ties, just the right amount of gray in his hair, and a smile that could have lit up about fifty percent of the houses in Pecan City any night of the year. Besides, he was happily married, had two daughters, and looked like the former track star he was. If he didn't exist, the Chamber of Commerce would have had to invent him.

He had a proposition for Burns.

"You've heard of Edward Street, of course," Miller said

when he had made sure that Burns was comfortably seated in one of the red leather chairs that furnished his office.

"Yes," Burns said, trying to get off his backbone. The chair was much too soft for sitting, and Burns was afraid he might disappear between the cushion and the back. He made it up and edged to the front of the seat. "He's the school's most famous former teacher, I guess, but he was gone before I came."

Though Mal Tomlin was fond of saying that no one had ever made less money by leaving HGC, Edward Street was the one former instructor who had really succeeded, thanks to a book of poetry, of all things, that Street wrote while on a year's sabbatical from teaching.

It was titled, *Dying Voices*, and it was composed of a series of dramatic monologues supposedly spoken by twenty-five great writers as they lay dying. Burns could not remember all the voices, but he recalled Keats, Byron, Shelley, Faulkner, Hemingway, Fitzgerald, Wolfe, Melville, Hawthorne, and Twain, among others. The fact that several of the men who spoke in Street's book had died quite suddenly and with very little time for final utterances made no difference either to Street or to the critics, who loved the book, which somehow, through an inexplicable fluke of divine providence, also caught on with the public like no book of poetry since the heyday of Rod McKuen, wound up on the best-seller lists, and was made into a highly-rated television mini-series.

Street followed up that unlikely success with the novel of high adventure that Burns suspected all poets really wanted to write. Titled *We All Die Today!*, it was the story of a young, idealistic graduate student (of English, of course) who was recruited by a Cuban friend to help him smuggle his family into the United States. The two went on their way, blithely unaware that the U.S. Government was about to launch something that became known as the Bay of Pigs at the very same time, and of course the two plans collided with the predictably terrible results. The U.S. covered itself in shame, the Cuban family did not survive, except for one small girl, and the graduate student died in an incredibly noble and selfless manner. His final speech, as he lay bleeding on the beach from the multiple bullet wounds he had suffered from both Cuban and American weapons, was as moving as anything in *Dying Voices*, and when the book was translated to the silver screen, there wasn't a dry eye in the house at the climax.

Street became a millionaire with that one, and he never returned to teaching. Since that time he had been involved in any number of projects, including movies and television, and his name was quite familiar to Burns, who had seen it many times on screen.

Sometimes Burns wondered if he envied Street, and he had decided that he probably did.

"So what I think we should do is this," Franklin Miller said. He had been speaking all through Burns's reverie about Street, and now he was about to come to the point. "I think we should honor the man, concentrate on *Dying Voices*, naturally, since that's the thing that has the most, ah . . . *academic* appeal. We'll have a few visiting scholars in, let them present papers on the book, that sort of thing. We can get national publicity on this if we do it right, Burns."

Burns had been around long enough to realize that the two *we's* in that last sentence, though they were the same word, did not mean the same thing at all. The first "we" meant Franklin Miller, and possibly HGC; the second "we" meant Carl Burns.

But that didn't necessarily bother Burns. He knew that someone had to do the work and someone had to get the credit. And that the two someones were hardly ever the same.

He also suspected that publicity was not the only thing involved here. Anyone with a big bankroll, and Street certainly fit that category, was fair game for Miller's fund-raising activities, especially if that person had ties to HGC.

That didn't bother Burns, either. The more money the school had, the better his chances for a raise. If Street could be flattered into parting with a decent sum, Burns's chances were improved with every dollar.

So of course he had said, "It sounds like a great idea to me."

"Excellent," Miller said. "Excellent. My secretary will get in touch with Street, find out when he's available, and we'll leave it to you to make all the other arrangements. We'll call it something like 'The Edward Street Seminar.' Have a banquet in his honor, that sort of thing."

They had shaken hands and Burns had gone back to his office to start making lists and worrying.

Now, after a little more than three months, everything was as ready as it would ever be. Four fairly reputable scholars were coming in to read papers. The news media had been alerted. Miller had handled that part. A big banquet of welcome for the former teacher had been planned, invitations issued, a menu arranged.

What could possibly go wrong?

Nothing, probably, but that was where Burns's list came in. He was a habitual worrier, and a habitual list maker, so the two habits fit together well. He was able to write down all the potential problems that he could think of and then eliminate them before they arose.

That was the theory at least. Unfortunately, most of the problems were purely imaginary, and the ones that weren't were not the kind that could be solved in advance. Nevertheless, it was a comfort to Burns just to have the list.

Burns looked down at what he had written on the piece of paper. It was pretty straightforward:

1. No one will want to read a paper.

2. If anyone does want to read a paper, the papers won't be acceptable.

3. We won't be able to get anyone to come to a seminar on such short notice.

4. Street will hate the whole idea.

5. No one in the department will want to work on the project.

6. If we get the project off the ground, no one will show up for the seminar.

7. People will want to come, but they won't be able to get here because Pecan City doesn't even have an airport.

8. Miller won't be able to sell the idea to the faculty.

9. There will be a lot of resentment against Street from some of the older faculty members.

10. There won't be any publicity.

Actually, even Burns had to admit, most of the problems weren't even real. There weren't many papers submitted, true, but those that came in were good. There might have been more had he been able to call for them sooner, like a year in advance, but the only weekend Street had open was the first one in September. So that was that.

The faculty had been enthusiastic, and any old feuds or resentments, if there were any, had been buried deep, or at least well hidden. The English department had pitched in eagerly, even Miss Darling, who remembered Street as "a really dynamic young teacher." Of course, anyone under the age of seventy was regarded as young by Miss Darling.

Street himself liked the idea. He had never returned to the HGC campus in the nearly twenty years since his leaving, and he was looking forward to being there again and visiting the few old acquaintances who still remained on the faculty.

And Pecan City did have an airport of sorts, with regular shuttles to both Dallas/Ft. Worth and Houston.

Even the news media were cooperating, though Burns had yet to see the notice Miller had hoped for in something like *Time* or *Newsweek*. Still, the seminar had been mentioned in one of the Dallas papers, which also planned to send a reporter. There was at least still a small chance that they would hit the big time.

So Burns put the list back into his drawer, more or less satisfied.

It never occurred to him to add an eleventh item to his list of worries, the item that would guarantee national publicity and insure that HGC would get its name in all the best papers and even on television.

After all, he had no way of knowing that someone intended to kill Edward Street.

· 2 ·

He still had five minutes left before class began, so Burns decided to give Maintenance a call on the off chance that someone had gotten there early. He looked up the number in his campus directory and punched it on the new beige telephone that was installed in his office over the summer. No one in the administration was saying how much the up-to-date new and improved phone system had cost, but rumor (and HGC thrived on rumor) had it that it was the reason no one on the faculty had received a pay raise.

After all, technology has its price.

However, in spite of the lack of a raise, there was no question that the new system was capable of wonderful things. Both call-forwarding and call-waiting were available. You could transfer calls to other offices, and you could even have conference calls with people both inside and outside the system.

Of course to do those things, you had to learn a complex system of "flash hooks" and symbol-punching that no one, with the possible exception of Franklin Miller's secretary, was going to take the trouble to learn. Anyone wanting a different office from the one he or she had gotten on the first try was just going to have to hang up and go back through the operator, and most people didn't want to be called if they weren't in their own offices, so the call-forwarding feature was worthless.

So naturally there were some of what Dean Elmore, whose idea the new system had been, would have called "soreheads," who thought that it was an extravagance. But they would never have said so out loud. Not all fear of reprisal had died with the dean.

The phone had rung five times, and Burns was just about to hang it up when he heard an answer.

"Maint's."

It was Clarice Bond, the Maintenance secretary. She had a beehive hairdo and wore glasses like the women in Gary Larson's cartoons. She also had a complete inability to speak many English words without omitting a number of vowels and consonants, and she was not much of a conversationalist. Burns didn't like to talk to her on the phone.

"This is Carl Burns," he said. "I'm in my office in Main."

There was silence on the other end of the line. Burns could hear a vague humming noise on the wire, but that was all.

Burns plunged on. "There seem to be pigeons flying around in the attic over here.'

There was still no response.

"And the smell is pretty bad. Do you think you could get someone to do something about it."

"Th' sm'll or th' p'jins?"

"Uh . . . both," Burns said, hating himself for the use of vague pronoun reference.

"I'll t'll 'm."

Burns heard a click and realized that the conversation was over. He had no idea whether it had done any good, but he guessed he would find out. Anyway, it was possible that as the air conditioning began to cool things off for the day, the smell would go away. Or that it would at least become less noticeable. To save money in the summer, there was no air conditioning in Main. It was old and poorly insulated, and it was easy enough to move classes to other buildings, so the heat and the smell had built up over the last three months.

Burns gathered up the books and handouts for his class and wound his way through the maze-like halls, passing by the offices of Miss Darling and Clementine Nelson on the way.

Miss Darling had surprised nearly everyone by announcing her retirement during the annual fall workshop. She would be retiring at the end of the spring semester, she said, and then asked about whether the school's hospitalization policy would cover flu shots. Most people had thought she would die in her classroom at HGC, but apparently she was going to disappoint them.

She had not come in yet, her first class not beginning until ten, but Clem was there, just about to walk out the door. She looked even more severe than usual, her hair combed straight back, her face free of make-up, but Burns knew that she was one of the kindest, as well as one of the smartest, of HGC's faculty. She was old enough, and had been there long enough, to remember Street.

"Good morning," Burns said. "Ready to greet the leaders of tomorrow one more time?"

Clem smiled, looking less severe and showing straight, white teeth. "Lead on, MacDuff," she said, knowing that Burns would appreciate the slight misquotation. She collected the better examples of such things from her students' papers, and one of her favorites—as well as Burns's—had been written by one of her sophomores about Medea in Euripides's play of that name: "Hell hath no fury like a woman spermed."

As far as Burns was concerned, that just about said it all. "I want to talk to you after class," Clem said as they walked toward the classrooms. "About one of the papers for the seminar."

"Trouble?" Burns asked.

"I don't think so. I've just been wondering about it."

"I'll see you after class, then," Burns said. He hoped that she hadn't come up with something that would cause them, or *himself*, since he was the one to whom the dirty work would fall, to have to call the reader and say that they had rejected the paper at this late date. It was bad enough that they had only four.

He went into the classroom at the head of the stairs. He always assigned himself that particular room because it was large, had windows on two sides, and seemed to have the best air conditioning of any on the floor. He was the chairman of the department, and rank had its privileges, though very damned few of them.

There were thirty-four students scheduled for the class, and Burns found that only one was absent when he called the roll. That was a good sign.

He carefully explained all the items on the handout and then asked if there were any questions, an empty formality if there ever was one. There were never any questions.

He looked at his watch. He had used precisely forty-five minutes. Good enough.

"That's it, then," he said. "You have your assignment sheets, so you may now go buy your books and get started on the reading. See you all tomorrow."

The ones who hadn't closed their notebooks ten minutes before, only a few, did so now, and the class broke up. It was only the first day, so there was not the great rush there would be later in the semester when anyone pausing in the doorway was quite likely to be trampled.

Burns waited until everyone had left before making his own exit, just in case a question had occurred to someone.

It hadn't.

He walked around to Clem's office and waited for her. She was much better at keeping her classes the whole time on the first day than he was. She had a lot more experience.

The office was furnished with a blonde desk and chair that really didn't look very good with the institutional green of the walls, but then neither did any of the other office furniture in the department, all of which was a dark mahogany. Burns had no idea where the blonde furniture had come from. For all he knew, Clem might own it.

There was also a blonde captain's chair, which Burns sat in to wait, and a blonde wooden filing cabinet. Burns's own filing cabinets were gray steel, and he wondered how Clem rated a wooden one. Maybe she *did* own the stuff.

Clem came in right after the bell rang to signal the official end of class. Burns got up so that she could get by him to her desk. The office was so small that there was hardly room for him, her, and the blonde furniture.

Clem put her books down and they both sat.

"What's the problem?" Burns asked.

"It's that paper by Melinda Land," Clem said. "The one called *'Dying Voices: Art or Artifact?'*"

"Oh," Burns said. "That one." To tell the truth, it had worried him, too. A little. Land was a professor at the University of Houston at Clear Lake, an upper-division and graduate school near NASA, and she had obviously done quite a bit of study on Street's work. Her title referred to the question of whether Street's poetry was really poetry (in the literary sense) or merely a form of popular verse that would be forgotten within a few years after its creator died, like most of the work of certain other poets who were lauded in their own lifetimes. Longfellow, for instance.

"You think she was too hard on the book?" he asked. The professor did ask some hard questions, but her conclusion was that the poems stood up to most of the tests for good, if not great poetry, and would quite possibly outlive their creator. There was a certain irony in that, which Burns could not appreciate until later.

"No," Clem said. "I was wondering if she was too easy on it."

Uh-oh, Burns thought. Clem could be as tenacious as a pit bull if she believed a matter of principle was involved.

"Too easy?" he said.

"I was wondering if she came down on Street's side just so she could read her paper. There's a lot of pressure on those people at big schools to read papers. They need to do it for tenure. Maybe she really thinks Street's poems are inferior verse. There's at least a hint of that in her paper."

"Let's give her the benefit of the doubt," Burns said. "Did you bring this up because you think the poetry's no good?"

"I don't know," Clem said. "I have to admit that there were times when her arguments against the poetry seemed stronger than the ones in favor of it."

"Do you think Street will be offended?"

"Probably not, if he was willing to come back here in the first place. He ought to expect a little bit of a tough time."

Burns had talked to Clem over the course of the summer about Street's tenure at HGC. Although she had not really gone into detail about it, she had never indicated anything that would have led him to doubt that Street's time there had been anything but happy. He began to think about the list in his desk drawer.

"Why should he expect a tough time?" he said.

"Well, when he was here, not everyone thought he was quite as wonderful as he thought he was. He always had an exaggerated idea of his own importance, or it seemed exaggerated at the time. I suppose that he turned out to be pretty important after all, but those of us who were here then remember him as a little bit of a blowhard. And not all the reviewers had been kind to his work."

"Miss Darling liked him."

"That's the way she remembers it now."

Burns tried to draw her out, but that was all he was going to get. Clem didn't like to gossip.

"It wouldn't really be gossiping," he said. "I need to know things like that. What if I seat him next to the wrong person at the banquet?"

"I'm sure that won't happen. Now if you'll excuse me, I have to be going to class."

Sure enough, as she stood up, books in hand, the bell for the nine o'clock class rang.

Burns stood and let her by, then followed her into the hall. He didn't try to persuade her to say any more. He had enough things on his mind, and maybe there was really nothing to worry about. No one had indicated any hard feelings in the planning sessions.

He took his books and papers to his office and dumped them on his desk. It was time to head down to the History lounge.

Burns, Tomlin, and Earl Fox, chairman of the History Department, had arranged their schedules so that they would all have a free period at nine. They planned to meet at that time on the second floor in the small room that they had claimed for their lounge.

They didn't have much of a claim, but then they didn't need one. No one else wanted the room, which had not been remodeled along with the rest of the building in the early nineteen-seventies.

It still had an eighteen-foot ceiling, and the single light hung down on a frayed fabric cord. The old card table and folding chairs were still the only furniture, and the walls had not been painted since the early years of the century.

There was one new decorating touch this year, however. Earl Fox, who could not stay away from a garage sale any more than Bugs Bunny could avoid Elmer Fudd's garden, had somewhere located a cheap plastic imitation of a Tiffany shade. He had gotten a stepladder from the utility closet on the first floor and attached the shade to the dangling light cord, giving the room the appearance of the waiting room of the cheapest whorehouse in the world.

The room was already filled with smoke when Burns entered without knocking, scaring Fox into tossing his cigarette to the floor. Fox loved to smoke, and he loved to try a different brand with every pack he bought, but he didn't want anyone in the HGC administration to know that he smoked. He thought that by throwing the cigarette to the floor and ignoring it, he could fool anyone who happened to catch him at it.

Today he was smoking Cost Cutters from Kroger; the yellow and white pack was lying on the card table's peeling top. He picked up his cigarette when he saw that the intruder was only Burns.

"I wish you wouldn't do that," he said, knocking imaginary—or possibly not-so-imaginary—dirt off his cigarette. He was wearing a Hawaiian shirt that looked like one of

Thomas Magnum's cast-offs, a pair of greenish double knit slacks, and Reebok running shoes that looked as if they had been run in for about five thousand miles. Burns had always suspected Fox of buying his clothes at the same sales where he found such irresistible bargains as the Tiffany shade.

Burns sat in one of the folding chairs. He sat carefully, just in case the chair decided to collapse under him, but it held his weight without a tremor.

"Want a smoke?" Fox said.

"I quit over the summer," Burns said.

"That's what I told him," Mal Tomlin said. He was also seated at the table, but he had continued to smoke calmly when Burns entered. He didn't care who knew he smoked. "I told him about the pigeons, too."

"If it's not rats, it's pigeon shit," Fox said, flicking ashes in the general direction of the center of the card table. "I don't know what this place is coming to."

It was then that Burns noticed another new decorator touch—an immense purple glass ashtray in the shape of a leaf. Or maybe it was a flower.

"Nice," Burns said, indicating the ashtray.

"Yeah," Fox said. "Thought I'd try to class up the place a little bit, give it that homey touch. I was tired of the alligator one."

"You did good," Tomlin said. "About those rats, by the way. I haven't seen any hint of them since the last one. I kind of miss it. Gave the place character."

The rat to which he referred had become known as The Rat. It had died the previous year in the men's room gasping its last between a board and the stone wall behind the toilet. Only its tail and feet had hung down, causing consternation to both Fox and the building's maid, Rose, who had refused to remove it.

"I guess they poisoned all of them," Fox said. "I'm glad to be rid of them, myself."

Burns thought about the poisoned rats. He wondered what Maintenance would do about the pigeons. Not poison, surely.

"Speaking of poison," Tomlin said, taking a puff on his Merit, "how's the Street seminar coming along? You got everything under control?"

"I suppose so," Burns said. "Why'd you bring it up in connection with poison?"

"Free association, I guess. I overheard somebody at the workshop talking about Street and saying that his name was still 'poison' in some quarters around here."

Burns felt a prickle of cold sweat pop out on his back. Suddenly he wanted a cigarette very much. But he resisted the urge.

"Who said that?" he asked.

"I don't remember. It was just something I heard in passing. You know, I was passing by a bunch of people and somebody said it."

"Nobody said anything like that to me," Burns protested. "Everyone I've asked has been very helpful about the seminar." He was thinking of what Clem had just told him, however. It was beginning to appear that not everyone had been exactly truthful.

Earl Fox laughed and scattered ashes all over his colorful shirt. "What did you expect people to say? Everybody knew that Dr. Miller was behind this thing a hundred percent. Surely you didn't think anyone was going to cross him, did you?"

Burns shook his head.

"Of course not," Fox said, crushing the Cost Cutter in the new purple ashtray. "There may be a new administration, but some things just don't change. Besides, half the faculty's hoping Miller will appoint them Academic Dean, and they're all staying on his good side. Elmore may be dead, but he's still causing trouble."

It was true. The College Board had decided to let the new president pick his own second-in-command, and many of the current faculty hoped that Miller would choose from among the ranks. Their theory was that the devil you knew was better than the devil you didn't. Burns liked to remind anyone who said that about the last dean chosen from among the ranks—Dean Elmore, one of the biggest mistakes in the school's long history.

"So you think there might be some underground opposition to honoring Street?" Burns said.

"I'd say so," Tomlin answered. "But that's just what I'd guess from what I heard."

"I wish you could remember who said that," Burns told him.

Tomlin tried, through at least three more cigarettes, but he couldn't recall, so they all trooped downstairs to see where the pigeons were getting into the building.

It was easy to spot the place, or places, since there were plenty of the birds busily engaged in flying in and out.

"They should have taken better care of those windows," Tomlin said, stating the obvious.

He smiled at Burns. "Right over your office, too."

It was true. Burns's office was stuck out on the side of the building in what might have at one time been planned for an elevator shaft. Above it was a sort of bell tower that had never housed a bell and in which there were several tall windows, all of them with broken panes.

"I wonder how those panes got broken," Fox said.

Tomlin lit a Merit with a green Bic disposable lighter. "I bet it was that storm we had last year right at the end of school."

Burns and Fox nodded. That had to be it. There had been a tremendous thunderstorm with lightning and considerable hail. One of the windows in Burns's office had been broken, and his books on that side of the room had gotten soaked.

That window had been fixed, but apparently no one from the maintenance crew had noticed the panes in the windows up above. Not that Burns blamed them. He hadn't noticed, either.

They went back up to the History lounge so that Fox could have one last smoke before ten o'clock, when they all had class again.

"Did you call about the pigeons?" Tomlin asked.

"Yes," Burns told him. "I talked to Clarice."

"Ah," Tomlin said. He had talked to Clarice before. "I hope they take care of them before the seminar. I'd hate to see a guest on our campus getting shit-a-cosis."

"Can you get that from pigeons?" Fox asked.

"I don't know," Burns said.

"I bet you can," Tomlin said darkly. "And God knows what else. There'll be a ton of fresh shit up there in a month."

On that jolly thought the nine-fifty bell rang, and they broke up the first History lounge meeting of the year.

· 3 ·

The week had gone by quickly and about as smoothly as first weeks ever do. There was only one disturbing incident, and that had nothing to do with the seminar.

Friday afternoon, Burns hung around Main much later than was his usual habit, or anyone's usual habit for that matter. After one o'clock on Friday, it was virtually impossible to find anyone in the building except for the occasional student-secretary who had been left behind to answer the telephone and cover for everyone who had left, which was everyone. Well, Rose, the maid, was there, but she had to be. Her job description called for her to work from seven until four.

The general feeling among the HGC faculty was that they would teach day and night, Monday through Friday morning, but that Friday afternoon belonged to them. As did Saturday and Sunday, of course.

As Mal Tomlin liked to put it, "There has to be *some* reason to get a Ph.D., right?" Friday afternoon was that reason for a lot of people, including Burns. It was what made all the years of graduate school worth the trouble.

On the Friday before the seminar, Burns was to meet Edward Street at the Pecan City airfield at 4:30. Not really having time to go home and relax, Burns decided to stay in his office and get a little ahead in reviewing his texts and note-taking for his classes. He didn't really have any grading to do, not that early in the semester.

As usual, he got sidetracked into list-making before the afternoon went on for long. Tomlin and Fox were already gone, so there was no one to meet in the History lounge, and the English faculty had left right after lunch, so Burns was practically alone in the building.

Bunni, his student-secretary, was there, but she was at the desk in the hallway that ran in front of the three offices occupied by Larry, Darryl, and Darryl, as the other three male English teachers were called. Burns had learned to transfer his calls to the phone on the desk where Bunni worked, just in case anyone ever called on Friday afternoon. As far as he knew, no one ever had.

The list he was working on was a particularly troublesome one that he called "Great American Writers That No One Ever Heard Of." He didn't like the title in the first place, because a lot of people had heard of the writers on it. He thought of changing it to "Great American Writers No One Thinks Are Great." That might be better.

It was Burns's theory that there were many novelists who had written very good books (though not great books, he had to admit that, and he thought he would have to take that part of the title out or change it, too) books as good as those read in most of the classrooms where American literature was taught.

But whereas everyone would agree that Norman Mailer was an important writer, no one wanted to talk about James Gould Cozzens and *Guard of Honor*, much less writers like John D. MacDonald and Ross Macdonald, both of whom, Burns was convinced, had written books every bit as good as a lot of Hemingway, most of Mailer, and almost all of Truman Capote.

He had begun the list three times, torn it up and started over, when he heard noises in the attic.

It wasn't the pigeons. He had already gotten used to the pigeons. This was much louder, and it was clear that someone was up there. There was a lot of tromping around by what could only have been human feet, followed by a frenzy of beating wings that sounded almost like thunder.

Then he heard the gunshots, or at least he thought they might have been gunshots. He hadn't had enough experience to be sure.

The pigeons were going wild, and Burns was about to go see what was happening when Bunni came running into his office.

Bunni in full flight was a sight to see; she jiggled delightfully in all the right places, and Burns had to keep reminding himself that she was promised to George ("The Ghost") Kaspar, an HGC football player. She was also so many years younger than Burns that he often told himself that her mother was more in his own age bracket, which was a painful truth that he didn't dwell on any longer than absolutely necessary.

"Dr. Burns!" she shouted. "Dr. Burns!" There's something going on in the attic!"

Bunni had a talent for stating the obvious, and she also chewed gum, two more reasons why Burns's fantasies about her never lasted for very long. And of course there was her name. Even if she had been as old as Burns, there would have been the name.

"I noticed the noises, Bunni," he said, trying to be as calm as she was excited. He was older and had to keep up at least the appearance of serenity in the face of the unknown.

"Do you think . . . I mean, can you . . . well, ..."

The noise was right overhead now, and dirt and feathers were filling the air. "I think I'd better see what's happening," he said. He didn't want to stay in there much more than Tomlin had, though he didn't share Mal's fears of parrot fever.

He and Bunni both went out into the hall and down to

the storeroom door, which stood open. There was a note taped to the door that said

PLeAse!
Keep THis!!
Door!!!
LockeD!!!
MAiD Rose

Rose had taped the note to the door almost a year ago, and this was the first time since then that Burns had seen the door open.

At the back of the storeroom was the stairway that led to the attic. Burns was about go investigate, when he heard someone coming down the stairs. He and Bunni backed away to see who it was.

It was a boy about eleven or twelve years old, carrying some kind of rifle. He was followed by a wolfish-looking man whose thick black hair was combed back on the sides of his head. He had a distinct widow's peak, like Eddie Munster. He was carrying a black plastic trash bag.

"Who's that?" Bunni whispered.

"Mr. Fairly," Burns said. "He's the Maintenance Supervisor, and that must be his son."

"What's he got in that bag?"

"I don't know," Burns said, which was the truth, although he had a pretty good idea. He just wasn't going to tell Bunni, unsure how she might react.

"It's probably just trash," he said, but he suspected that it was something else.

Dead pigeons.

Burns had not felt like accosting Fairly, so he sent Bunni back to her desk with the assurance that the attic had just needed a good cleaning.

He went back to brush up his office as best he could before going to meet Edward Street.

He got to the airfield, ten miles out of town and a relic of a World War II Army camp, just in time. Street had arrived and was ready to be driven to his motel.

For Burns, it was not a fortunate meeting. For some reason, he took an instant dislike to Street.

Maybe it was the way the man dressed. Like Franklin Miller, Street had been a college track star. Unlike, Miller, he had never gotten over it. He was wearing a royal blue silk warm-up jacket with the name "Speed" embroidered in red over his heart. "Speed" had been Street's college nickname, and he apparently still used it, though he looked anything but speedy. In fact, he looked as if he might die of heart failure if he had to do anything more energetic than type a line of poetry.

He was about five feet seven or eight inches tall, and he must have weighed a hundred and eighty pounds, with a lot of it concentrated in the stomach.

He had a round head, and Burns thought immediately of Charlie Brown, except that Street had thin black hair that looked dyed and probably was, considering the man's age.

When Burns introduced himself, Street tried to crush his hand and very nearly succeeded. Maybe all that fat was really muscle, Burns thought, trying not to give any indication that his hand felt a little like a horse had stepped on it.

"Glad to meet you, Burns," Street said. "Those are my bags." He pointed to two giant brown Samsonite leather bags near the car rental desk. "Where's your car?"

Burns showed Street the 1967 Plymouth Fury III, and though the writer looked astonished, he didn't say anything. He just went outside and got in, leaving Burns to get the bags.

Burns told himself that he didn't mind and that, after all,

Street was a guest. He picked up the bags, though it was hard to grip the one in his right hand, and staggered outside, wondering if Street had brought along his entire wardrobe. Or perhaps two bags of bricks. He was sure that he was going to have a strained back from carrying them.

Fortunately, the Plymouth, in addition to being able to seat eight adults, had a trunk in which you could hide a small elephant. Burns hoisted the bags in one at a time and slammed the lid. He didn't even have to lay the bags over on their sides.

"Hell of a car," Street said when Burns got in. "I have a Porsche, myself."

"Umm," Burns said, starting the Plymouth. There was a loud roar — the car needed a new muffler — and a large puff of white smoke came from the tail pipe.

"Looks like you could use a ring job," Street said.

"Umm." Burns put the car in drive and started back to town.

Street made himself comfortable on the wide front seat. "I bought the Porsche right after *Dying Voices* hit it big. I figured I deserved it. Some people like diamonds, I wanted a Porsche."

"Right," Burns said, concentrating on the road. "That certainly sounds reasonable to me."

"Of course I never could have afforded it on my salary at good old HGC," Street went on. He was the type who apparently didn't need much encouragement when it came to talking. "I don't suppose they're paying any better these days, are they?"

"Probably not," Burns said.

"Didn't think so. But at least it's a job. Better than nothing. I could have done a lot better for myself after *Voices*, naturally. Plenty of schools will pay to get a famous writer on the staff just to teach one class. But I thought I'd try one more book, see where that got me. Boy am I glad I did."

"You don't miss teaching then?" Burns asked.

Street gave Burns a sideways glance, snorted, and then laughed aloud. "Don't try to kid me, Burns. You know you'd jump at the chance to quit. Anyone would. Spending your life correcting comma splices for people who don't give a damn, trying to teach the difference between a fragment and a sentence to kids who'll never write anything any more ambitious than a letter to their mamas, and who won't do that if there's a telephone within reach — what kind of life is that? No thanks."

Burns was tempted to argue, but he didn't. He had to admit that Street had a point, but there was something about teaching, or trying to teach that Burns liked, something that he would miss if he left the profession, or at least that's what he told himself, despite the fact that he would not really have minded owning a Porsche.

"I know what you're thinking," Street said. "But it's bullshit. You wouldn't miss those students for more than five minutes, I promise you. You can do all the lecturing you want to at writers' workshops if you need the ego boo."

Burns didn't think he needed ego boo. He thought he just liked to teach. There was something, after all, about seeing someone, even just *one* someone, catch on to an idea, or learn to write a complete sentence, or suddenly discover that he loved to read poetry after having told his buddies for most of his life that poetry was for sissies.

He couldn't tell any of that to Street, however, and Street probably would not have believed him anyway. Street got his pleasure from other kinds of things.

"You know," he was saying, "I told myself after I left HGC that I'd never come back, even if *Dying Voices* was a total failure. Maybe especially if it was a failure. I don't think I could have faced that. People around here always treated me like some kind of freak, just because I was a real writer, like most of them wanted to be if the truth were known, instead of someone who wanted to spend his life grading the writings of semi-literate cretins. The only place they ever got published was in some little magazine with a circulation of about ten. I promised myself I'd never return unless I was invited and unless I could come in style."

"Miss Darling told me you were a dynamic teacher," Burns ventured.

"Is that old bat still around? My God, she must be a hundred and ten. Or older. She was practically senile when I was here."

"She's still doing a fine job," Burns said, moved to defend Miss Darling even if what Street said was uncomfortably close to the truth. Last spring Miss Darling had tried to check her gradebook in at the library circulation desk, insisting that it was overdue.

That was only a momentary aberration, however, and it hadn't caused much of a fuss, since the head librarian had been on duty at the time and had told no one except Burns. The librarian had retired in the spring, and Burns was quite interested in the replacement, a certain Miss Tanner.

"Well, it's good to hear that Miss Darling is still doing well," Street said insincerely. "How about old Don Elliot?"

Elliott was the chairman of speech and drama, a short, shriveled man with an impressive voice. He had done fairly well for himself in HGC terms, having what amounted to free room and board for himself and his wife, in addition to their salaries. In Street's terms, however, that would be next to nothing.

"He's doing very well, too," Burns said. "His students did a fine job with last year's musical. *Oklahoma*. They'll be doing a Shakespeare play this year."

"I'm sure it'll be wonderful," Street said. "Poor old Don always thought he was going to be the next Olivier. I bet he never thought *I'd* be big in Hollywood."

He was silent for a minute, then said, "That was some doings you had with Elmore last year, wasn't it?" Burns didn't know how to take that. Did the "you" mean Burns specifically, or did it mean the school?

"Too bad Elmore got knocked off," Street went on. "He was a fine guy. One of the best. He and I always got along."

If Street was a friend of Elmore's, Burns thought, that explained a lot. He had never before met anyone who liked

Elmore but somehow he wasn't surprised. The two men were a lot alike. Elmore, however, was not one of Burns's favorite topics, and he decided that it was time to change the subject.

"What did you think of the papers we received for the seminar?" he asked. As a courtesy, he had sent copies of the papers to be read for Street's perusal.

"Didn't read them," Street said. "I quit reading stuff about myself a long time ago. I never believe any of the bad things, and the good things just give me an inflated opinion of myself."

He was trying to sound modest, as if he didn't really mean that it was possible for his ego to be inflated, but he couldn't quite pull it off. Burns wondered if he was lying about having read the papers.

Street looked as if he might have had more to say on the subject of whether he read about himself, but there wasn't time. They had arrived at the motel.

Burns was just as glad. It had been a long ten miles, and he wasn't looking forward to the banquet that night at all.

·4·

When Burns thought about it later, especially when he was feeling uncharitable, he wished that Street had been killed before the banquet. It would have saved everyone—except Street, who appeared immune—a lot of embarrassment.

For one thing, there were the books.

That was what had made the bags so heavy, numerous copies of *Dying Voices* and *We All Die Today!* Street brought them to the banquet and shamelessly hawked them to all his old acquaintances and to anyone else who would give him a chance.

There was nothing Burns could do but stand back and listen. He didn't feel that he could ask the guest of honor to stop selling his wares, even if he was acting like a television huckster for diet pills.

"Don, Don Elliott, how in the world are you? Gosh, it seems like only yesterday that we were sitting in the faculty meetings and griping about the salaries. How'd you like to have an autographed copy of *Dying Voices*? Not a first edition, of course, those are worth their weight in gold these days. Hell, there were only two thousand in the first printing.

How was anyone to know that a book of poetry would be a genuine cultural phenomenon? But this one's signed, and I'll let it go for publisher's list, no charge for the autograph.

"Why, Miss Darling, what a charming hat! I didn't know that women even wore those things any more. I know a refined teacher of English like you admires good writing of any kind. How about a copy of *Dying Voices* of your very own?

"Land? *Melinda* Land? The one who wrote the interesting paper on my work?" *The one you said you hadn't read*, Burns thought. "Well, I'm sure you have copies, but they're probably all marked up. Don't you want fresh ones?"

It was pretty bad. Street was doing everything but offering to accept major credit cards, and Burns would not have been surprised to hear him do that. He had raised self-promotion to an art form.

And then there was the whiskey, which had apparently been in the bags along with the books.

Whiskey was pretty hard to come by in Pecan City, and in fact, one of the few liquor stores in town liked to advertise its "convenient drive-up window, located in the rear of the store," the perfect answer for the people—and there must have been many of them—who didn't even want to be seen buying liquor.

As a former resident, Street had come prepared.

The problem was that the banquet was being held in the school's only large dining facility, which was on the ground floor of the men's dorm. Liquor was expressly forbidden in any of HGC's buildings.

Burns had not been aware that Street had the whiskey until the banquet was beginning, when the writer pulled the fifth of black-label Jack Daniels out of the same bag from which he had been dispensing his books.

While Abner Swan, the chairman of the Bible Department, was asking the blessing—a task that usually required about five minutes, unless Swan was in a particularly expansive mood, in which case seven to ten minutes were necessary—Burns saw Street fishing around in the bag, which he had stashed beside his chair.

He came up with the whiskey and poured it into his tea glass. He had already drunk the iced tea, leaving only a small amount of ice in the glass. He didn't seem to require a mixer.

The clinking of glass on glass sounded to Burns like the last trump. He glanced furtively around, hoping to see only piously bowed heads, but it was obvious that the attention of many of the diners had wandered during Swan's lengthy blessing, and a number of them were watching Street in fascinated horror.

President Miller was one of the watchers.

Burns had not met anyone's eyes, so he bowed his head and tried to appear incredibly reverent, meanwhile wondering about the possibility of job openings in Outer Mongolia.

The interminable blessing (six minutes by Burns's estimate) was followed by excellent prime rib, not the usual fare in the dining hall. Burns was sorry that he couldn't really enjoy it.

After the eating came the speeches.

Miller welcomed Street to the campus after his years away, though Burns suspected that the welcome had been toned down somewhat in the time since Miller had seen Street's private stock.

Then Don Elliott recalled the days when Street had been his colleague and congratulated him on his great success.

Burns got up and spoke for a few minutes on the next day's activities. The papers would be read beginning at nine o'clock on the first floor of Main in room 101, a large lecture hall. Everyone was welcome to attend, and after the papers were read there would be a panel discussion of Street's works in which Street himself would participate. Burns was tempted to add, "If he doesn't have a hangover the size of his suitcase," but he managed to restrain himself.

Through all of this, Street looked quite happy to be the center of attention, and indeed he looked even more than merely happy. He seemed to swell visibly in what he must have interpreted as the approbation of his former colleagues, and he continued to suck contentedly at the contents of his tea glass. It reminded Burns of the despised and rejected high school nerd returning as a millionaire to a class reunion.

After Burns's remarks came the part of the evening that Burns had been dreading ever since meeting Street at the airport. It was Street's turn to speak.

Another little problem with Street was that he had not changed clothes. He still wore the blue silk jacket with his nickname in red and a pair of faded jeans.

There wasn't anything wrong with that, but Street had to know that at HGC, although perhaps not in the rest of the world, banquets were taken very seriously. Everyone dressed to the nines, or what passed for the nines in Pecan City.

Abner Swan, for example, had clothed his ample form in a tuxedo for the occasion and looked to Burns like a slightly less demented and much larger Burgess Meredith in his appearances as the Penguin on the *Batman* television show. Without the cigar, of course. All the other men were wearing dark suits and ties, even Burns, who hated ties, and the women were decked out in their Sunday best.

Burns found himself quite interested in the clothing of Miss Tanner from the library. She was wearing a clingy dress of some kind of man-made material, which Burns found most enticing. In fact, he found Miss Tanner most enticing in general. She had honey-blonde hair and big green eyes that seemed even bigger because they were magnified by the lenses of the huge round glasses she wore. Burns hoped that he might get a chance to talk with her later, but right now he had to worry about Street, who was having some difficulty in getting up. The iced tea was always served in large glasses at HGC.

But Burns needn't have worried. After only one false start and a bit of awkwardness, Street made it to his feet and started talking.

He rambled a little at first, understandably, considering the amount of liquor he had consumed, and talked about how he had never forgotten his humble origins, although he had made it bigger than anyone listening to him could ever hope to do, lacking his generous helping of talent and, though he hated to be the one to say it, genius.

Then he really got started.

"I thought, at one time, I'd have to spend my life grubbing along at third-rate colleges, that I'd never get out of Pecan City. But I did. I made it on guts and drive and talent. I look out over this group of people, and I see some who have been here twenty-five years. Or more. And they'll never go anywhere else. Never know what it's like to have fame and money. Well not me, buddies. I know what it's like, and I love it."

He went on to tell them what it was like.

Flying first class instead of tourist.

Ordering whatever he wanted to eat at whatever restaurant he wanted to eat in.

Being on a first name basis with any number of famous movie and television stars.

Never having to worry about the size of your bank account at the end of the month.

"Money is freedom," he said. " It's power. It's wonderful."

He sat down to a mild applause. Very mild.

Burns glanced at Miller who was glaring at him. Burns had the sudden feeling that the Edward Street Seminar was now all his idea and that Miller would be telling everyone that he was amazed that Burns had ever thought of it in the first place.

At least there was no one from Newsweek *there*, Burns thought. Unfortunately, there was someone there from one of the Dallas Papers. Burns was sure he would be blamed for that, too, though all publicity had come from Miller's office. Then he chided himself for thinking such a thing. Miller, after all, was not Elmore.

As people began to leave, very few of them came by to speak to Street as they had been doing before the banquet. For his part, Street didn't seem to care very much, and he dug around in his suitcase, getting out several copies of his books and piling them on the table in case any prospective customers presented themselves.

The next day's speakers, whom one might think would

be interested in meeting the man whose work they so closely studied, were clearly keeping their distance.

Even Mal Tomlin and Earl Fox headed for the exits. Burns vowed silently that he would make them pay for deserting him.

But Miss Tanner walked over.

Burns was sorry to see her coming. Not that he hadn't wanted a chance to speak to her, but he didn't want to have to talk to her in the presence of Street.

Street, on the other hand, was delighted, his delight no doubt influenced somewhat by the liquor he had consumed.

"Best-looking woman I've seen all day," he said. "Surely you don't teach at this godforsaken place."

"I'm the head librarian," she said. She had a deep, husky voice, and Burns wondered if she was a smoker.

"A librarian," Street gushed. "I love librarians! I'm sure you have copies of my books in your stacks, but do you have copies of your own? I'm sorry I can't offer you a copy at a library discount, but then I don't get that good a deal from the publisher when I buy my own copies. The autograph is free, though."

Burns wanted to hit him.

"I already have copies," Miss Tanner said, to Burns's disappointment. "I love your books."

Street stood up a little straighter and tried unsuccessfully to suck in his stomach. "I—" he began, but he was interrupted by the reporter from the Dallas paper.

"Mr. Street?" the man said. "My name is Harold Duncan. I'm a reporter for—"

"A reporter?" Street said. The gleam in his eye that Miss Tanner had inspired increased in intensity. Street was the kind of man who liked reporters even better than librarians.

"That's right," the man said. "A reporter." He was a short, unattractive man with sparse brown hair that he had fluffed up to make it appear thicker. He was holding a notebook and a pen in nicotine-stained fingers.

"I always love talking to reporters," Street said. He must

have been telling the truth. He didn't even try to sell Duncan a copy of either of his books.

"Good," the man said. "I'd like to take a little of your time and ask a couple of questions."

"Fine," Street said. "Fine. Ask anything you'd like."

"First of all, I think my readers might like to know about a letter we received at the paper several days ago."

"Letter?" Street said, obviously puzzled. "I don't know anything about any letter."

Burns didn't like the sound of this. There was some kind of insinuation in the little man's voice. He looked at Miss Tanner, and she had caught it, too.

"Yes," Duncan said. "A letter which claims that you are not the true author of *Dying Voices.*"

Street's face, already red from the black Jack, changed to mottled purple.

"That's outrageous! That's . . . that's . . ."

"That's what the letter alleges," Duncan said. "Would you care to comment?"

"I'll comment, all right. That letter is full of bullshit! Just absolute bullshit!"

Several people who had been standing in the doorway, looked back inside at the sound of Street's raised voice. Franklin Miller turned and started back to see what was going on.

This is great, Burns thought. *Just great.* He looked at Miss Tanner, who didn't seem to have been offended by Street's language. In fact, she was almost smiling.

"What seems to be the problem here?" Miller asked, arriving on the scene without having heard exactly what Street had said.

"No problem," Duncan said. " I was just asking Mr. Street about the allegation that he is not the author of *Dying Voices.*"

"What?" Miller was nonplused. "What allegations?"

"They're contained in a letter received by my newspaper two days ago," Duncan said.

"I want to see that letter!" Street bellowed. "I demand to see that letter!"

"We will produce it at the proper time," Duncan said. "You're standing by your comment that the allegation is 'bullshit'?"

"Of course I am, and you can print that. It's bullshit."

Miller looked around to see if anyone had overheard. "Bullshit" was not a word that HGC faculty and administration bandied about in their conversations, at least not in public.

"Very well," Duncan said. "I'll be looking forward to your panel discussion tomorrow." He folded his notebook, in which he had not written, and turned to leave.

"You come back here, you little slug," Street said. "You come back here and I'll stomp you to jelly!"

"Bad idea," Burns said. "You can't just stomp reporters to jelly and get away with it."

"Who's responsible for that little bastard being here?" Street said, obviously not seeing any humor in the situation. "I'll have his balls, by God."

Another vague reference, Burns thought. Did "his" refer to the reporter or to whoever invited him there?

"We have a free press in this country," Miller said, covering his ass. "There's no way to keep reporters out."

"Well, he'd better not be there tomorrow if he doesn't want his butt kicked," Street said. "That's all I've got to say."

He turned to Burns. "Get me out of here."

"All right," Burns said. "I'll get your suitcase."

"The hell you will." Street went back to his chair and got his own bag. It was almost as if he suspected that Burns might steal the whiskey, now that he knew it was there.

"Interesting man," Miss Tanner said.

"Do you think there could be anything to what that reporter said?" Miller asked.

Burns had no idea, and said so.

"Who would send a letter like that?" Miller wondered. "I just can't believe anyone would do that."

Burns didn't have any answers for him, but he intended to ask Street as soon as he got him in the car.

"I have a feeling that this seminar might turn out to be more interesting than I thought," Miss Tanner said.

"Let's go, Burns," Street said. "I want to get out of here."

"I'm sorry this happened," Miller told him. "I'm sure he won't cause any trouble tomorrow."

"He'd better not, if he knows what's good for him," Street said. "I'll kill the little prick."

"Please," Miller said, looking around, whether because of the death threat or because Street had said "prick" Burns wasn't sure.

Burns took Street's elbow and guided him out of the room.

· 5 ·

Street had nothing to say to Burns during the short ride
to the motel, and Burns couldn't think of a polite way to ask
him what was going on, so he simply dropped him off and
told him that he would pick him up at eight-thirty the next
morning.

Street grunted and slammed the door. "Those bastards
will be sorry!" he yelled over his shoulder as Burns drove
away.

Burns went home and watched the ten o'clock news and
went to bed, but he didn't sleep well. He was too worried
about the next day.

Street was not waiting for him when Burns arrived at the
motel in the morning, so Burns parked the Plymouth and got
out. He knocked on Street's door, but there was no answer.
Thinking Street might have overslept, Burns knocked harder.
There was still no response.

He checked the restaurant, in case Street had gone in for

breakfast, but Street was not there. There were mostly locals, drinking coffee and eating watery scrambled eggs.

Burns went back to the room and knocked on the door again, getting a little worried now. Good grief, what if Street had gotten so mad he had left town, just taken off without a word to anyone?

Still no answer.

Burns began to sweat, thinking of other horrible possibilities. Street had drunk a lot of liquor at the banquet, and he might have continued to drink after getting to his room.

What if he was still asleep in there, deep in the throes of alcoholic dreaming, so deep asleep that Burns would not be able to wake him? Worse yet, what if Burns could wake him, only to find a man with a hangover so bad that his eyebrows ached?

What if he was so hung over that he couldn't get himself together to appear at the seminar?

Well, whatever the case, Burns had to find him first.

Burns went to the desk and explained his problem. The clerk checked the computer and discovered that Street had not checked out. Then she called the manager, who agreed, somewhat reluctantly, to let Burns into the room.

"He might be sick," Burns argued. "Or hurt." He didn't mention the hangover idea, which probably came under the heading of "sick," anyway.

Burns and the manager, a short, bald man with a sour face, walked back to the room. There was more knocking on the door, this time by the manager, but the result was the same: no answer.

The manager put his pass key in the lock and turned the knob. The door would not open.

Uh-oh, Burns thought.

Apparently the manager thought the same thing. Somehow he got the key to work and opened the door.

Street was there, all right, still wearing his blue jacket. He was lying sprawled across the still-made bed, an insignificant-looking spot of red on his forehead. The Jack Daniels bottle was in one hand, the remains of its contents having run out onto the bedspread to cause a dark stain.

There was another dark stain, too, this one behind Street's head. It was suddenly obvious to Burns that Street would not be attending the seminar, nor anything else in this life.

"Oh, shit," the manager said, his mouth twisting and causing his face to look even more sour than before.

Burns didn't say anything. He just stood there and stared.

Boss Napier, the Pecan City Chief of Police, did not appear happy to see Burns again.

"It seems to me, Burns, you got a bad habit of finding dead bodies," he said.

"This is only the second one," Burns said, worried because Napier had gotten his name right. The chief hardly ever got names right, and Burns was sure that his doing so in this case was a bad sign.

They were sitting in the room next to Street's, which happened not to have been rented out the previous night. It looked just like Street's room, except that it was reversed. The rug was the same dull orange, as was the bedspread. Even the print on the wall—purple mountain's majesty—was the same. Burns could hear the evidence crew, or whatever it was, in the room next door.

"So you brought him out here last night and left him," Napier was saying. He was a big man, with short blonde hair and blue eyes. He wore a white Western-style shirt that was tight through the shoulders and around the stomach, brown jeans and brown boots. The chief didn't have to wear a uniform. Everyone in Pecan City knew who he was.

"You got any witnesses to prove you went straight home like you said?" he asked.

"No," Burns said.

"And I don't guess you have any idea who killed this guy?"

"No," Burns said again. He was sitting in one of the uncomfortable chairs by the cheap Formica-topped table. "I'd tell you if I did."

"I guess you would at that," Napier said, "considering all we've been through together. What I can't understand is how you wimp English teachers keep getting mixed up in stuff like this."

"It's not because we want to," Burns assured him.

"Yeah. Well, tell me about this little seminar thing you've got going on."

There had been quite a bit about the seminar in the newspaper, but Burns didn't mention that. Maybe Napier had read about it and was simply checking to see if what he had read was accurate.

When Burns had finished explaining, Napier said, "So it's going on right now?"

"Yes," Burns said. "I called Clementine Nelson and told her to take my place."

"She going to tell them about Streak?"

"Street. Edward *Street*. No. She's just going to say he can't be there for the panel discussion."

"Well, she won't be lying." Napier walked aimlessly around the small room, looking at the walls and the furniture. He stopped for a second to admire the snow-topped mountains in the picture. "You think maybe one of those out-of-towners killed Streep?"

"Street! And I don't have any idea." Burns hadn't even considered that possibility. As far as he knew, none of the people reading papers for the seminar had ever met Street. Most of those in attendance at the seminar, except for the readers, would be HGC faculty who had felt a good bit of pressure from Miller to attend.

"I hope you aren't thinking about getting mixed up in this," Napier said.

"Believe me," Burns told him, "it's the farthest thing from my mind."

"Hah," Napier said. "That's what you said the last time."

"It was true the last time, too. I got involved against my will."

"Yeah, and you like to've got dead. I hope this time you'll stick to teaching that *Julio Caesar* and leave the detective work to me."

"I will," Burns promised. He meant it. He had not liked what had happened to him the last time he got involved with murder, though of course it was impossible not to speculate a little about why someone whose body you've found might have gotten killed.

So he asked Napier, "How did he die, anyway?"

"Shot with a small-caliber gun, probably a .22," Napier said. "You know anybody's got one of those?"

"No," Burns said, but he was thinking about the gun Fairly's son had been holding. That was probably a .22. Burns was no gun expert, however, so he decided not to say anything.

"Probably knew the killer," Napier went on. "At least he let him into the room and was still drinking in front of him."

"Or her," Burns added.

"Sure, or her."

"So I'll have to check on your speakers and everybody at the school who knew Street or had met him as soon as we get through going over the room."

"If you count the people at the banquet last night, that's a lot of people."

"Well, that's what we get paid for. Anything funny happen at the banquet that you want to tell me about?"

Burns told him about the reporter and the mysterious letter.

"Oh, fine. That's real dandy. I wish you'd told me that a little sooner. Now we got a motive. All I got to do is find that letter. I hope this Dunphy is a cooperative type."

"Duncan," Burns said. "I'm sure he will be," he added, though he was sure of nothing of the sort. Duncan looked like a lot of things, but cooperative wasn't one of them.

"He better be," Napier said, and Burns was reminded of all the stories he'd heard about the man, about his bullwhip and the secret wrestling hold he was reputed to use on particularly recalcitrant prisoners and his .357 magnum, which, to tell the truth, Burns had never seen him wear.

"You think he'll be at that seminar thing?" Napier asked.

"He probably wouldn't miss it, not if it would give him a chance to confront Street about the letter again."

"My men can finish up here," Napier said. "I guess we better go down to your seminar and meet Dunbar. And those folks who came to town to read their papers, too."

"My car or yours?" Burns said.

"Both," Napier told him.

They got there just as Melinda Land was finishing her paper. There was mild applause, and most of the audience of about thirty people turned to see who had come in the door. When the HGC faculty saw Boss Napier with Burns, the applause stopped altogether.

Melinda Land, an attractive red-haired woman of about thirty-five, looked out across the audience to see what was going on.

Burns walked up to the podium and joined her. "I hate to interrupt," he said. He looked out at the audience. Fox and Tomlin were there. So was Miss Tanner. Clem, Miss Darling, and Larry and the Darryls were there as well.

So was President Miller, whom Burns was sorry to see. He had hoped the president might have skipped out early.

"I know that most of you were looking forward to a panel presentation that we should be having now, right after this last paper," Burns said, "but we won't be having it after all."

No one looked too disappointed, but everyone looked extremely curious, especially the president. Burns had asked Napier about what to say at this point.

"Tell 'em the truth. You think if you keep murder a secret, somebody'll crack under the strain and confess? It won't happen that way, Burns. This isn't *Barry Mason*."

So Burns told them the truth.

"Edward Street is dead. He was murdered in his motel room."

There were gasps in the audience, looks of shock. Miller put his head in his hands and shook it slowly. Harold Duncan, sitting on the back row, got out a notebook and started scribbling away madly. Burns was certain that the seminar had suddenly become extremely interesting to at least one person.

Melinda Land, still standing beside Burns, put out a hand and touched his arm. "How . . . how did it happen?"

"Chief Napier of the Pecan City Police is here with me," Burns said, more to the audience than to the woman beside him. "He'll give you any further information that he can." That meant none at all, but Burns didn't say so.

Napier strode to the front of the room, and Burns stepped away from the podium.

"I'm going to have to talk to each one of you individually," Napier said. "Dr. Burns tells me we can use the classroom next door for the interviews. I won't keep most of you very long, and we're going to start with the back row and work our way to the front. I know this is inconvenient, but we have to get it done. Now is as good a time as any. Burns will send you in one at a time."

Several people tried to get Napier's attention to ask him questions, but he ignored them, walking to the back of the room and out the door.

"Please stay in your seats," Burns said loudly. Everyone was getting up, talking, pressing toward the front of the room to speak to him. "Chief Napier doesn't want me to say anything more about this right now. He'll tell you as he interviews you. Please sit down so that we can do this in an orderly manner."

No one sat down. It struck Burns, not for the first time, that teachers were very bad about behaving in just the ways that they did not allow their students to behave. He felt as if he were dealing with an unruly class of high-schoolers.

He slipped his college ring around until the synthetic

ruby stone was facing down and then banged on the hard wood of the podium with it. The room got quiet.

"Please sit down," he said. He waited for a minute, until they had done so. "Thank you. Chief Napier is ready, I'm sure." He looked at the back row. "Mr. Duncan, you can go first."

The reporter looked as if he might argue, but he didn't. He got up and went out of the room.

Burns looked at Melinda Land, who was still there next to him. "You can sit down," he said. "This might take a while."

"All right," she said. She took a seat on the front row.

Burns started to go and sit with Tomlin and Fox, but there was a vacant seat by Miss Tanner. He couldn't resist, even though out of the corner of his eye he saw Miller beckoning frantically.

"How were the papers?" he asked as he settled himself in the chair.

"Interesting," she said, looking at him with her big green eyes. "But not as interesting as your morning, I'll bet."

"Probably not," Burns agreed.

She glanced around. Clem Nelson was sitting on her left, but Clem was talking to Miss Darling, who still appeared to be in a state of shock.

"I want to talk to you after all this is over," Miss Tanner said. "In the library."

Burns resisted the urge to look over his shoulder to see if there was someone there. He could hardly believe that Miss Tanner wanted to talk to him, though it really wasn't so surprising. He was the center of attention, all right. But in the library?

"I thought the library was closed on Saturday," he said.

"It is," she said. "But I have a key."

"Oh."

"There's something I want you to see."

Burns's mind immediately indulged itself in a wild flight of fancy. "I think it might have something to do with this murder," Miss Tanner said, spoiling the fun.

"Oh," he said again. "Shouldn't you tell Chief Napier about it, then?"

"It may be nothing. Besides, I'd rather show it to you first."

Burns remembered what he'd told Napier about getting involved. Then he looked into Miss Tanner's green eyes. "I'll meet you there as soon as we're finished here," he said.

A heavy hand landed on his shoulder. *Oh, God,* he thought, *Napier's already caught me.*

But it wasn't Napier. It was Franklin Miller.

"I want to talk to you, Burns," Miller said. "Now."

"Of course," Burns said. "Of course." He got up and walked with Miller to the side of the large room.

"I want to know what the fu— what's going on here." Miller said. His voice was strained and tight. "Is this some kind of monstrous joke?"

"I'm afraid not, sir."

"Good Lord. Do you know what this means?"

Probably a lot better than you do, Burns thought. "No, sir," he said.

"It means a tremendous black eye for the school, that's what it means," Miller said. "How do you think this is going to make us look?"

"I hadn't given it much thought, to tell the truth," Burns said.

"Well, you'd better think about it. Edward Street murdered! At our seminar! Holy shi— my gracious! We'll be the butt of gossip all over the state."

"I expect Street feels pretty bad about that," Burns said.

Miller glared at him. "Is that a joke, Burns?"

"No, sir."

"It had better not be. This isn't funny. It isn't funny at all."

Burns was going to say that he didn't see anyone laughing when Duncan stuck his head in the doorway.

"Next," he said.

·6·

It irritated Burns no end that he still thought of the library as Hartley Gorman III. He had always hated the designation of the buildings by number, a practice loved and encouraged by the late, unlamented Dean Elmore. And when the administration building had been destroyed by a fire, Burns had rejoiced to think that the numbering system had been rendered obsolete and even useless. Which it had. No one other than Elmore had ever cared for it or used it, and Miller apparently didn't want to take the time to learn it.

But now, for some unaccountable reason, Burns couldn't get the numbers out of his head. He supposed that when a new administration building was built—not one of the school's priorities—things would be easier on him. The new building would not have, would never have, a number.

The library itself was not anything to brag about, neither because of its architecture nor its holdings. To tell the truth, many of its volumes—too many in Burns's estimation—had come from such sources as former professors who, looking for a tax dodge or some such thing, donated all their books to the library upon their retirement. Thus there were many old and useless volumes, which, despite the fact that they helped inflate the book count in reports to accreditation associations, did no one any good at all.

There were also a great many—again, in Burns's mind, far too many—old textbooks. Professors at HGC, being too morally upright to do as many of their colleagues at other schools, refused to sell their desk and examination copies to the buyers who frequently came by offering tax-free cash on the spot for textbooks. Instead, everyone gave the books to the library, thereby clearing their own shelves of books that they would never read and once more increasing the library's holdings by a sizable number of books that no one else would ever read, either.

Miss Watts, the former librarian, had tried to "weed" the library every now and then, sending out notices to department chairmen and asking them to come by and check the stacks for outdated materials. Burns did his job conscientiously, but he wasn't sure how many others did. And besides, Miss Watts was erratic in what she might choose to do when the time came, no matter what was suggested to her, as Burns had reason to know.

One thing the library did have, something that Burns enjoyed very much, was a large collection of nineteenth-century magazines, donated by some long-dead patron, probably from a personal collection. The magazines had been bound and preserved quite well in the library. Burns liked to browse through them occasionally, but one day he had been walking to the mail room by a route that led him behind the library and he had happened to look into the large dumpster there.

What he saw horrified him, and he climbed into the dumpster, first looking around to see whether anyone was watching. He knew that he was about to go dumpster-diving, and he didn't particularly want any of his students to see him. No one was watching, fortunately, it being about 11:15, a prime time for classes.

Once inside the dumpster, he found that his eyes had not tricked him. He was standing on a thick layer of bound volumes of the *Atlantic Monthly* dating from the previous century. He opened one and flipped through it to an excerpt from Twain's *Life on the Mississippi,* the first publication of that work.

He forgot all about his mail and climbed out of the dumpster to go and confront Miss Watts, who calmly informed him that all the material in the cast-off periodicals had been transferred to microfiche; it was no longer to be allowed to take up valuable shelf space. The bound volumes themselves were nice, but by no means necessary.

Burns did not yell. "But you're taking up space with the second printing of *The Harbrace College Handbook,"* he said. "Not to mention the third, fourth, fifth, sixth—"

"Our students need to learn about commas," Miss Watts said. "You, of all people, should know that, Dr. Burns."

"But those books were probably last checked out ten years ago," Burns protested.

"They are there if the students need them, however," Miss Watts told him.

He tried again. "But these are valuable research documents you've thrown away, the original printings, just like someone in the Nineteenth Century might have bought them and read them."

"And they are preserved exactly like that on the microfiche," Miss Watts said, pressing her thin lips together.

Burns knew when he was licked. He slunk back out to the dumpster, climbed in, and tossed out all the volumes that were there. Later he got Tomlin and Earl Fox to help him carry them up to the third floor of Main, where they still sat on the shelves of a seldom-used classroom, along with the back issues of Burns's copies of *Rolling Stone,* documents of questionable historical value, he thought, but ones that certainly would not be found on Miss Watts's microfiche.

Nor would you find there that other legendary HGC hoard, or what had once been a legendary hoard. Pecan City's only claim to literary fame before Edward Street was a writer who made a small fortune writing under his own name and various pseudonyms for the pulps in the 1930s, churning out stories for magazines with titles like *Spicy Detective, Thrill-*

ing Detective, Ten Detective Aces, and *Ranch Romances.* He had died of a heart attack at the age of forty, and his mother had donated his considerable pulp collection to the HGC library, where her son once was a student.

Miss Watts had been at the school even then, and she had objected strenuously to the covers of the magazines, which generally featured scantily-clad young women in some frightening situation that had little or nothing to do with the stories inside. Miss Watts had been more or less obligated to accept the gift, but she had stored the magazines in the darkest, most spider-infested reaches of the damp basement of Main, where they had rapidly deteriorated. Burns had found their remains during his first year at HGC, the old pages gnawed by rats and silverfish, crumbling to fragments at his touch. He'd never quite forgiven Miss Watts for that, either.

Seeing the library with Miss Tanner would help me get a new perspective, he thought. He was sure she would be progressive and yet eager to preserve the past. He waited outside until Boss Napier had questioned her and they left Main together.

"He's a very nice man, isn't he?" Miss Tanner said.

"Who?" Burns said. "Boss Napier? A nice man?" She must not be talking about the police chief, but there hadn't been anyone else in the room with her during the questioning.

"Yes, Mr. Napier. He seemed very polite and concerned. Sort of handsome, in a rugged way."

Burns glanced at her glasses out of the corner of his eye. Maybe she needed to have the prescription changed. He could hardly believe what he was hearing, and he didn't pursue the topic. He was almost afraid to.

"What's this about the library that you wanted me to see?" he asked.

"I'll just have to show you," she said.

It was not far from Main to the library, and they walked the rest of the way in silence, Burns puzzling over her remarks about Napier and wondering what the library held.

The library was a red brick rectangle three stories high, resembling very much the incinerated Administration Building, except that for some reason it had a porch front that resembled the entrance to a Greek temple, complete with Corinthian columns. There had once been flowerbeds in front of the library, but Dean Elmore had purged them when he purged the honeysuckle in front of Main.

Burns and Miss Tanner mounted the five steps to the cement porch, and Miss Tanner unlocked the glass doors, known for some reason as the "E. R. Memorial Doors," perhaps in remembrance of some generous donor now known only by his or her initials. They stepped into a small glass foyer which protected the library from the weather outside and from which they could see the large entrance room of the library. Miss Tanner then unlocked the inside doors.

When they entered the library, the circulation desk was to their right. It had been moved near the doors from the stack area to prevent students from stealing books, something that happened with appalling regularity even at a moral place like HGC. From their perch behind the desk, those in charge of the desk supposedly could give the students the evil eye and cry out if anyone tried to walk out with a book that had not been properly checked out. It was an inefficient and mostly unsuccessful system, but Dean Elmore had long ago decided that it was a lot cheaper than any security system that he could have bought. Maybe Miss Tanner could convince Miller to change things.

"We'll have to go back in the stacks," Miss Tanner whispered.

"All right," Burns whispered back. Like most people of his generation, he was well-trained. He always whispered in libraries.

The stack area was on the left, through another set of glass doors. The upper floors could be reached by way of either a stairway or an ancient Otis elevator that Burns suspected was none too reliable. Since the periodicals took up almost the entire first floor, with the exception of the space devoted to study tables, Burns knew they would be going up, and sure enough, Miss Tanner headed for the elevator.

"Miss Tanner," Burns said.

"Elaine," she said. "My name's Elaine."

The fair lady Elaine, Burns thought, as visions of Arthurian damsels danced in his head and he mentally measured himself for a suit of shining armor.

"I'm Carl," he said, his heart thumping. He felt like an adolescent, but it wasn't a bad feeling.

"What were you going to say, . . . Carl?"

"Uh . . . uh . . . ?"

"Carl?"

Burns shook himself. He was a mature adult, after all. "The elevator," he said. "I'm not sure it's safe."

"It seems fine to me," she said. "I don't like to climb stairs."

They opened the outside elevator door, pushed back the accordion door inside, and entered the elevator. Miss Tanner pushed the button marked "3," and somewhere from within the depths of the building there was a grating, grinding noise. The elevator began to ascend, shaking slightly as it inched its way upward.

Finally it reached the third floor. Burns slid back the folding door and Miss Tanner pushed the outer door open. The dimly lit stacks of books were in front of them.

Burns liked books, even those old, outdated books in their mostly tattered bindings, their pages yellowing, their contents mostly irrelevant to current education. He liked the way they smelled in the hot, airless library, the way they looked on the shelves, short and tall, fat and thin, the way they felt in his hand when he took them down to look at them.

"They're up here," Miss Tanner said.

"What's up here?" Burns asked.

"The books," she said.

"What books?"

They were still whispering, their voices hardly carrying in the musty air because of the way the stacks broke up the sound.

"Street's books," Miss Tanner said. "Come on." She

started walking down the rows of stacks, her shoe heels clicking on the cement floor.

Burns followed her. On the end of one of the stacks he saw a penciled sign: "Beware of stack vampires."

"Uh . . . ," Burns said.

Miss Tanner stopped and looked back. "What?" Then she saw the graffiti. "Oh." She laughed. "Don't worry about that." She took his arm and led him to the next row and pointed.

Someone had penciled "Sprayed for stack vampires, 2/21/86." The date had been crossed out and beneath it "3/11/87" had been printed. That had also been crossed out and below it someone had printed "3/28/89."

"I see what you mean," Burns said. "I guess everything's all right, then. Who does the spraying?"

"I have no idea," Miss Tanner said. "But I haven't seen a single stack vampire since I've been here." She tugged his arm. "The books are right down this row."

She turned and took two steps down the row. Then she reached up and pulled down two volumes.

Burns knew what they were immediately: *Dying Voices* and *We All Die Today!*

"Those are Street's books," he said.

"That's right. Let's go over there by the windows."

On the other side of the stacks were tables where students could make notes from the books without having to check them out from the library. There were signs posted on the wall by each table: PLEASE DO NOT RESHELVE BOOKS. LEAVE THEM ON THE TABLE.

Miss Tanner put the books down on the table with a thump. The windows were covered with half-closed Venetian blinds. Sunlight slanted through the blinds and across the books.

Miss Tanner opened *Dying Voices*. "Look," she said.

The pages to which she had turned were covered with something that looked like blood. It was bright red in the slanting sunlight.

"Shit," Burns said. Then he looked around guiltily.

"Don't worry, I've heard the word before," Miss Tanner said. "Just look."

Burns looked. As Miss Tanner flipped through the pages, he saw that they were all covered with splotches of the red color, which obscured the words on most of the pages.

"What is that stuff?" he said.

"I don't know. I came in here this morning to get the books before the seminar. I thought I might get Street to autograph them for us, if he'd do it for free." She looked thoughtful. "I wasn't sure he would, though. Anyway, I flipped through them and saw that they were both like this."

"Did you tell Boss Napier?"

"No. I . . . I wasn't sure whether he needed to know or not. I hadn't looked at the books before. I don't even know when this . . . vandalism was done."

Burns picked up the copy of *Dying Voices*. He looked in the back for the check-out record and pulled the slip from the pocket. "Somebody checked the book out last month," he said. "It must have happened since then."

"Unless whoever checked it out made the mess," she said.

Burns shook his head. "I don't think so. It looks . . . fresh." He looked at the check-out slip and tried to read the name which had been imprinted on it in purple letters. The name would have been printed from the faculty or student ID card of whoever had checked the book out, but Burns could not quite make out the words.

He moved the card into a better light, and then he could read the name. "Dr. Franklin Miller."

"Uh-oh," Burns said, not liking what he saw at all.

"What's the matter?" Miss Tanner asked.

"Look," he said, pointing to the name with his index finger.

"Oh. Well, it's only natural that he'd be curious about our guest, isn't it?"

"You'd think he would have read the books before now," Burns said.

"I suppose, but—" Miss Tanner looked around. "Did you hear that?"

Burns had heard nothing. "What?"

"I thought I heard something from the stairway. It must have been my imagination."

Burns put the check-out slip down on the table and looked down the aisle formed between the tables and the stacks. Suddenly the sunlight seemed dimmer than before.

"I don't see anything," he said.

"The stairway's over by the elevator," Miss Tanner pointed out. "You can't see it from here."

"Of course," Burns said. "I knew that." He wondered if she wanted him to go over and check out the staircase. That shining armor he had measured himself for was suddenly feeling a little tight. "I'll go look," he said.

"Never mind. It was probably nothing. Let's see if anyone checked out the other book."

She picked up *We All Die Today!* and began leafing through it. Burns could see the red stains spreading across the pages.

Just as she was about to pull out the slip in back of the book, there was another noise. This time, Burns heard it too.

"Someone's in here," Miss Tanner said.

"Did you lock the doors downstairs?" Burns asked.

"No. I thought that on Saturday no one would even try to get in."

"Probably just a student, someone who wants to get started early on his term paper," Burns said. "You do open on Saturdays later in the semester, don't you?"

"Yes," she said. "But I don't think it's a student."

"Maybe not," Burns said. He didn't really believe it, either. "Who's there?" he called out.

There was no answer.

"Maybe we'd better go now," he said.

Miss Tanner did not agree. "I can't leave the library unattended, not with someone sneaking around in it. We've got to find out who's up here."

"What if it's a stack vampire?"

"Very funny," Miss Tanner said, but she wasn't laughing. "I'll go down this row. And you walk on down about three tables and go down that one. Maybe we can catch whoever it is."

Burns didn't think much of the idea, but there wasn't anything he could do. He didn't want to look like a wimp English teacher to Miss Tanner, or even to himself.

"I don't think you should go alone," he said.

"Don't worry about me. I can take care of myself. It's probably just a prankster."

She sounded completely confident, a lot more confident than Burns felt.

"All right then," he said. "But yell if you need any help."

"I will," she said, but he didn't think she would.

· 7 ·

Burns usually liked the feeling he got when he was alone in the old buildings at HGC. He liked listening to the sounds they made, and he liked the feeling of freedom and timelessness he experienced.

This time was different, however. It wasn't that Burns believed in stack vampires, but suddenly the library did not seem a friendly place.

He had heard the stories, which he had also heard at other schools, about the kinds of people libraries sometimes attracted. It was told for truth that one of HGC's more unusual students had developed a method of sexual harassment that he perpetrated in the library. Burns could not recall the student's name, if he had ever known it, but the young man was supposed to have waited until the stack area was deserted and then cleared out the books from the bottom row of shelving, distributing them elsewhere in the stacks. He would then lie down on the floor and roll onto the shelf, where he would have an excellent view of the ankles of young women who walked by looking at the upper shelves. And if the women were wearing skirts, so much the better.

He had been caught one day when an alert student spotted him peering up at her cotton panties, but not before he rolled off of the shelf, bit her on the calf, and led the authorities, including an incensed Miss Watts, on a merry serpentine chase in and out of the rows and rows of shelving.

Burns hoped that the noise he and Miss Tanner had heard was caused by someone as relatively harmless as the stack-peeper, but he was a bit worried. After all, a man had been murdered and his books had been defaced, not the usual thing at quiet, peaceful HGC.

He wished that the lighting were better, but the stacks were not lit by the usual method. Each row of books had its own lights, suspended from the ceiling and covered with a milky-white globe. A string hung down from each light so that they could be turned on one at a time. All this was no doubt the result of some long-ago economy measure enacted so that no more than one light would be burning at once, so long as whoever turned it on remembered to turn it off. Miss Watts had been vigilant about the lights and usually had one student worker who was assigned to do nothing more than walk up and down the rows of books turning off lights that had been left burning.

Burns himself walked through the rows now, not turning on any of the lights but looking carefully down each row as he went. He did not see anyone. He did not hear anything, either, not even the sounds of Miss Tanner's heels clicking on the floor. Maybe she had taken off her shoes.

He was looking down the row labeled QL-460/RB-139 when he finally heard something, though not from the direction he expected. The noise came from behind him, a faint "shhhh" sound, as if someone had slipped a book from its place on the shelving.

He turned, half-expecting to see Miss Tanner, but he didn't see anything.

Or, technically speaking, he saw *something*, but it was nothing more than a blur heading straight for his face. He found out later that it was a book, but at the time he didn't really have a chance to examine it.

He experienced something like a really sudden migraine

as the book smashed into his forehead and nose, and then he felt something crush. The crushing was accompanied by a terrible crunching noise that echoed in his skull and that came almost at the same instant as the thud that the book made when it met his forehead.

What had crunched was his nose.

Burns did not yell. He couldn't yell effectively with his teeth clenched as tightly as they were, but he did manage a sort of pained groaning as he stumbled backward into the shelf behind him, his arms outstretched.

He hit the shelf with the middle of his shoulders, which wasn't so bad, and with the back of his head, which was. It was even worse than being hit with the book, since the shelving was made of metal.

There was no loud *clong* like the tolling of a cathedral bell as his head struck, though Burns later imagined there must have been. There was more of a noise like a dull *thonk*. But it was effective, and pain shot from Burns's head right down to his shoes.

He realized then that his eyes were shut tight, so he tried to open them and get a look at his assailant. That was when he realized that he was falling.

And he wasn't the only thing falling.

The shelf that he had hit, the seven-foot-high, God-knows-how-many-feet-long shelf, was falling, too.

Burns did get his eyes open, and they opened extremely wide, since what he saw was the shelf he had just passed, QL-460/RB-139, and that shelf was also falling.

I didn't hit that one, Burns thought, just before he realized that the shelf was not only falling but that it was going to fall on him.

The books were already sliding off the upper shelves and pelting him: red ones, black ones, brown ones, their covers opening as they fell like heavy birds that were trying to fly like eagles and were falling like stones instead.

The noise was terrible, not only because of the falling books but because the shelf Burns had toppled hit the next shelf, which had hit the next one, which—

Burns didn't want to think about it. He covered his face as the first books began hitting him and rolled to his right, trying to get out of the way of the shelf.

He stopped rolling when he hit a table near the windows, and he lay there face down on the cold floor for a second or two waiting for the noise to stop. He didn't want to see what was happening.

It was soon quiet except for the occasional sound of one or two more books falling over on their sides.

Burns still didn't want to look. He was afraid that who-ever had hit him might try it again, and his nose was hurting fiercely. It felt completely stopped up, and he could feel blood running out of it.

In fact, since his face was a few inches from the floor, he could *hear* the blood running out, or rather he could hear it as it dropped onto the cement with dainty splatters.

Someone touched him on the shoulder, and he was gal-vanized into action. He lunged upward, got to his feet and stumbled across piles of books. One of the piles collapsed and he catapulted forward. Luckily, he had his arms stretched in front of him so avoided a headlong collision with the library wall.

The wall brought him up short and gave him the oppor-tunity to turn around and face his adversary.

Burns was not much of a boxer, but he had read a lot of Hemingway and a bit of Norman Mailer; he had even read a book about boxing by Joyce Carol Oates. He brought his hands up into what he believed to be the proper fighting position.

"I didn't know you were a fighter," Miss Tanner said. She was standing there holding her shoes in her right hand.

Burns dropped his hands. "I'm not. I thought you were the guy who hit me." His voice sounded funny to him, as if he had a bad cold.

"Someone hit you?"

Burns looked at the devastation around him. Books were strewn everywhere in heaps of prose. Five shelves—he had been near the end of the stacks, thank goodness—leaned crazily on one another, the final one resting on the wall. Most of the books were under the shelves, but many of them had spilled out into the aisle. Burns noticed for the first time that the shelving was in six-foot rather than twenty- or thirty-foot sections, so that only the first part of each row had been toppled.

"I hope you don't think I did this all by myself," he said.

"Well, I wondered. There was so much noise, but I didn't see anyone else—why, you look awful!"

Burns put a hand to his face, on his upper lip. Not to his nose. He wasn't about to touch his nose. He was afraid that he might scream if he did, and he didn't want to do anything so unmanly in front of Miss Tanner. He suddenly thought of Boss Napier, who, Burns was sure, would never flinch at something as wimpy as a nose injury.

His fingers came away from his lip stained with blood. He glanced down at his jacket. It was stained too, and so was his tie. He brushed his lip with the tie and wiped off most of the blood, though a little more trickled out of his nostrils almost immediately.

"I didn't really mean that you look awful," Miss Tanner said. "But your nose does look kind of funny, bleeding like that."

Burns was glad there wasn't a mirror handy. He didn't want to see his nose any more than he wanted to touch it.

"I hope I'm not scaring you," he said.

"Oh. No. It's just that . . . well, never mind. What happened to you?"

"I told you. Someone hit me."

"Who was it?"

"I don't know." Burns told her what had happened. "He must have hit me with the biggest book in this place. It felt like an unabridged dictionary. I'd have gotten him if he hadn't hit me first."

"I'm sure you would have. I wonder what he was doing here, and why he didn't answer us?"

Burns thought of something else. Though it pained him to mention it, he said, "We keep saying 'he.' It could have been a woman."

"A woman could have done that to you?" Miss Tanner's eyes were wide behind her glasses. *They are certainly a nice shade of green,* Burns thought irrelevantly.

"Why not?" he said. He wondered if she might be thinking about Boss Napier. Burns was sure that no woman could sneak up on Napier and clobber him like that.

"No reason. But why would anyone do that?"

Burns didn't know the answer to that one. He started toward her, kicking aside a book or two as he went. *What the hell?* he thought. He was sorry for the mess, and he was even sorrier that the books might be damaged, but if they could fall on him, he could kick them. He looked, but he didn't see any unabridged dictionaries.

"Where are you going?" Miss Tanner asked.

"To get those books of Street's," he said. "I think we should show them to Boss Napier." He didn't mention that he wouldn't have a sore nose and that the library wouldn't be in such a mess if she had gone to Napier in the first place.

"I suppose you're right," Miss Tanner said, slipping her feet into her shoes and following him. "I don't know how I'm going to explain this to President Miller, though."

"Tell him you were weeding the library," Burns suggested.

Naturally the copies of Street's books were gone.

They looked on the table where they thought they had left them, and then they looked on the nearby tables. They looked on the floor and even back in the stacks, but the books weren't there.

"They couldn't simply have disappeared," Miss Tanner said in frustration. "Did I take them with me when I went to see about the noises?"

"No," Burns said. "And I didn't take them either."

"Then where are they?"

"I think whoever hit me took them away with him."

"But why? They weren't valuable or anything. They were first editions, of course, but they had been read a number of times. The spines were worn, they had a library stamp on the endpapers, they—"

"I don't think they were taken by a book collector," Burns said, interrupting her.

"But who else would want them?"

"Whoever stained the pages," Burns said.

"Oh. But why?"

"Because . . . well, I don't know why. But I can't think of any better explanation. Besides, I don't think that some maniacal bibliophile would sneak up behind me and bash me in the face with an unabridged dictionary."

"True," Miss Tanner agreed. "Book collectors are usually much nicer people than that." She thought for a second. "But what are we going to do about Mr. Napier?"

Burns didn't like to hear her say the police chief's name, and he found that he didn't want her to be the one to talk to the man.

"I'll talk to him," he said. "He'll be pretty upset that we didn't tell him about the books sooner, and I'm used to him. He knows I'm not scared of him."

"But why would anyone be scared of him?"

Burns was tempted to tell her a few of the rumors about Napier, but he decided against it.

"I can think of a few reasons," he said. "But don't let that bother you. If he wants to see you, he will, after I get him calmed down."

He didn't know how he was going to get Napier calmed down, and he didn't particularly look forward to talking to him, but it seemed like the least he could do. He felt in some way vaguely responsible for what had happened in the library.

"You'd better have someone look at that nose first," Miss Tanner said.

"I will. What about you?"

"I thought I might stay here and try to clean up some of the mess," she said.

"I don't think that would be a good idea," Burns said. "What if our visitor comes back? What if he had something to do with Street's murder?"

Miss Tanner thought about that. "Maybe I'd better just go on home," she said. "It's just awful to think that a visitor to our own campus has been murdered."

"It certainly is," Burns agreed. "That kind of thing could give us a bad reputation."

"I didn't mean that the way it sounded," she said. She had another thought. "Why don't we call the police and let them come to investigate? If whoever did this is still here, they can catch him."

Burns knew that she was right about the call, though he didn't have much faith in the second idea.

"All right," he said. "We'll go down and you can make the call. I'll wait until someone comes, and then I'm going to the Emergency Room." He hoped that Napier would not come in person, but it was doubtful that the chief would be going out on routine calls.

"Maybe we should call Campus Security, too," Miss Tanner said.

"Campus Security" was an old man known to the students, and the faculty, too, as Dirty Harry. He carried a .357 magnum that he was just as likely to point at an innocent bystander as at a criminal.

"We'll call the police," Burns said. "Let's leave Dirty Harry out of it."

They went back to the elevator and let it shiver and shake its way to the first floor. They locked the front doors, just in case the vandal was still inside, which Burns seriously doubted, and then they went into Miss Tanner's office, which was located in the rear of the building down a short, dark hall.

While she made the call, he looked around her office. Her diploma was on the wall behind her desk and it confirmed the fact that her name was Elaine and informed him that she had a Master's degree in Library Science from Texas Tech University in Lubbock.

Nothing unusual in that.

What was unusual was the trophy shelf on one wall. It had probably not been intended as a trophy shelf, Burns thought. More likely it had been intended to hold books, but that was not what it was holding now. It was covered with trophies.

Burns walked over to inspect them as Miss Tanner spoke to one of Pecan City's finest on the phone, trying to explain to him that she meant the college library, not the local public library. It seemed the police were having a hard time grasping the distinction.

Burns looked at the trophies. It was a mind-boggling array. In fact, it seemed that Miss Tanner had everything but a Super Bowl ring, and Burns would not have been surprised to see one of those.

There were tennis trophies, track trophies, volleyball trophies, bowling trophies, and even an archery trophy—among others. Some were small, not more than six inches tall, while others were enormous. There was one on the top shelf that must have towered eighteen inches tall. The number 85, in gold, stood between two red and gold pillars that supported a marble crosspiece. On the crosspiece there was another red and gold pillar surmounted by a gold figure of Winged Victory. On the marble base, the wording engraved on a gold plaque told Burns that the trophy had been awarded at the "KTTP Invitational, 1985."

Nothing else on the shelf was quite so impressive, but there were one or two curiosities, such as the fact that one of the bowling trophies had been awarded in 1956. Looking at Miss Tanner, Burns found it difficult to believe that she had been old enough to bowl in 1956. In fact, he was sure that she had not been.

She hung up the phone and turned to him. "They'll be here as soon as they can—if they can find the place," she said. She noticed his interest in the trophies. "How do you like them?"

"They're, uh, pretty impressive," Burns said. "I didn't know you were so talented."

Miss Tanner laughed throatily. Burns found himself wanting to make her laugh again, though he wasn't sure why she was laughing this time.

"They're all mine, too," she said.

"I see that there's one here that's, uh, well, pretty old," Burns said.

She laughed again. Burns was beginning to feel quite witty.

"I said they were mine. I didn't say how I got them."

Burns thought about that for a second. Since he'd already brought it up, he thought he might as well keep on with it. "How did you get them, then?"

"I bought them," she said.

"Bought them?"

"At garage sales, junk stores, places like that. People like those things when they win them, but after they've gathered dust a few years they get tossed out or sold. So I buy them."

"Why?" Burns said. He was genuinely curious.

"They make me feel good. Whenever something bad happens, or if I ever start feeling depressed, I just go out and buy myself a trophy. Then I feel good about myself."

For some reason, Burns found himself thinking about the Cowardly Lion in *The Wizard of Oz*.

"I usually don't tell people that," Miss Tanner said. "Most people don't look at them very closely, so I just let them think they're mine."

"Your secret is safe with me," Burns said.

"Thank you," Miss Tanner said, stepping closer to him and putting a hand on the sleeve of his jacket.

Burns's heart started beating a little faster and he started to say something just as someone began pounding on the glass doors in front of the building.

"I imagine that's the police," Miss Tanner said. "They certainly did get here in a hurry, didn't they?"

Burns, who imagined that in a real emergency the police might have taken hours to arrive, said, "They certainly did."

Miss Tanner looked at him again with those green eyes, and then she went to let the police inside.

·8·

Burns did not like hospitals, but his nose was really hurting by the time the young patrolwoman had given the library a thorough search and finished questioning him and Miss Tanner. He drove to Pecan City Regional Hospital and parked as close as he could to the Emergency Room doors, which swooshed open as he approached them. He always thought of *Ben Casey* when he went through doors like that.

There was a tall blonde man wearing a pharmacist's white coat walking down the hall, and he directed Burns to the Emergency Room itself. Burns stood at the desk and filled out the insurance forms and tried to ignore what was going on around him, though it wasn't easy.

Some young man had brought in his small daughter to have a gash in her chin sewed up, and the girl clearly was not pleased to be there. She was sniffling and crying and trying to pull away from him.

Worse, there was a young man sitting near the wall with what appeared to be a broken arm. His left arm was twisted at an awkward angle, and he was trying hard not to cry.

His parents were sitting next to him, trying to comfort him. His mother was crying and the father looked disgusted.

"Tried to slam-dunk a basketball," the father said. "He's not but five feet tall, and he tried to slam-dunk a basketball. I've told him a hundred times not to try stuff like that."

"I've done it before," the boy said, sniffling. "I got a real good vertical leap." He stood up. "I bet I can jump four feet straight up. You wanna see me?"

"Uh, no," Burns said. He didn't want to get involved in a family argument.

The boy bent his knees, crouching as if to soar ceiling-ward, but the man clapped a hand on the boy's shoulder. "You better get some sense in you, boy," he said. "You want to get another broke arm?"

"No," the boy said, sniffling louder.

"Sit down, then," the man said.

Burns had to wait about an hour, but finally the boy got his arm put into some sort of soft cast, after a great deal of unruly behavior and a little yelling. Then Burns got his turn.

"Hummmm," the doctor said as he examined Burns's nose.

Burns hated it when doctors said "hummmm." It never meant anything good.

"I'm afraid it's broken," the doctor said cheerfully. "We'll fix it up good as new, or nearly as good. You can tell everyone it's an old football injury."

The doctor laughed heartily. Burns did not join in.

When the doctor was finished, Burns looked like Geraldo Rivera had looked after the skinheads, or whoever it was, had pounded him, except that he lacked Geraldo's swashbuckling flair. Or maybe it was the sleaze factor he lacked. Anyway, he thought, what he really looked like was a wimp English teacher with a broken nose. The bandage sloped down the sides, making a sort of pyramid, and he wondered what Miss Tanner would think of it.

He also wondered what Boss Napier was thinking about now. He had probably been informed about the incident at the library, about which Burns had to admit that he and Miss Tanner had not told the whole truth to the patrolwoman. Well, they had told the whole truth as far as it went. They had answered all the woman's questions openly and honestly. They just hadn't volunteered any information, such as the name of the person who had last checked the books out.

Napier had told Burns not to get involved in the case, but Burns was certainly involved.

Napier wasn't going to be happy.

Burns decided to go on home and forget about it. When he got to his house he noticed the stringless basketball hoop that the original owner of the house had attached to the roof over the garage door. Burns thought about shooting a few baskets, but then he thought better of it. He already had a broken nose; no use trying for a broken arm. Besides, he didn't have a basketball.

Burns parked the Plymouth in the garage, went inside, and tried to relax. He put a couple of Merle Haggard albums on his turntable and sat down with a pen and paper to make a list of the ten best country songs of all time. After he had worked for a quarter of an hour, he had only five songs listed, and three of them were by George Jones. That hardly seemed fair, though "She Thinks I Still Care," "The Window up Above," and "He Stopped Loving Her Today," certainly qualified. The trouble was, he couldn't decide which one to put first.

The other two songs were by Haggard, and that didn't seem fair either. Burns was worried that he might be influenced by what he was listening to. After all, the idea of a list of great country songs without one by Hank Williams in the top ten was ludicrous.

He wadded up the list and threw it at the trash can across the room. It rimmed the can and went in, but even that didn't make Burns feel better. He tried starting the list over, but that didn't work, either.

He knew what was bothering him. He could even make a list.

Street's murder.

The missing books.

Whether Napier had learned anything from questioning the people that morning after the seminar.

Burns got up and turned off the record player. He knew he wasn't being smart, but he also knew he was going to have to talk to Napier before his curiosity drove him crazy.

He called the police station, but he was informed that Chief Napier was off duty.

"Where can I reach him?" Burns asked. "I'd like to talk to him about a case he's working on."

"The Chief don't work cases personally."

"He's working on this one. It's a murder case."

"Oh, yeah. That writer at the motel. He's workin' on that one, all right. You say you got some information about the murder?"

That wasn't what Burns had said, but he decided to play along. "That's correct."

"Hang on a second, then. Maybe I can put you through to him."

There was a series of clicks, dead silence, and then a ringing noise. The ringing went on for quite a while, and Burns was just about to hang up when a voice said, "Napier here."

"This is Carl Burns, Chief. I was wondering if—"

"Look, Burns, I know what you're wondering. You're wondering if I'm gonna bust your ass for getting involved in Stream's murder like I told you not to, that's what you're wondering."

"Well, that's not exactly how I would have phrased it," Burns said. "I was hoping—"

"You was hoping I wouldn't break your wimpy English

teacher body in about a thousand pieces, that's what you was hoping."

"No, not that, either," Burns said. "I thought maybe—"

"You thought maybe you could suck up to me and get me to lay off you, but it won't work. I warned you, Burns, and now you're gonna be sorry."

"Look," Burns said, sounding as tough as he knew how, "are you going to listen to what I have to say or not?"

There was a moment of silence at the other end of the line. Then Napier said, "All right. I'll listen. But make it good."

"I want to talk to you about the murder," Burns said.

"I told you not to get involved in that," Napier said.

"I didn't intend to," Burns said. "It just sort of happened."

"You remember what 'sort of happened' to you the last time, don't you?"

Burns remembered, all right.

"Well, then," Napier said, "what makes you think this time'll be any different?"

"It probably won't be," Burns admitted. "I've already got a broken nose."

"A broken nose, huh?" Napier did not sound sympathetic. "That's what you get when you stick it where you ought not to." He paused. "I heard you got in a little tussle."

"Tussle" wasn't exactly the word Burns would have used, but he didn't argue the point. "I want to talk to you about that," Burns said.

"It's Saturday," Napier pointed out. "I spent all morning interviewing people about a murder. Then I had to go over the evidence and talk to the doctor about the autopsy. Then I get a call telling me that you and Miss Spanner—"

"Tanner," Burns said.

"—that you and Miss Tanner were assaulted in the library and that some books are missing, books, it just so happens, written by the deceased guy in the Holiday Inn."

Actually, he wrote them when he was alive, Burns

thought. He didn't say it, however. Napier didn't seem like the type who would enjoy discussing the finer points of grammar.

"So I guess you do want to talk to me," Napier went on. "I guess you want to explain just what the hell anybody would want with those books and why they had red stains all over 'em in the first place. And maybe you want to tell me how in the hell you got your nose broken."

"I think that about covers it," Burns said.

"It damn well better. I was gonna have you brought in, anyway, so I guess you can tell me and save the trouble."

Napier sounded a little disappointed to Burns, as if he had been looking forward to having Burns brought to the station. In cuffs, no doubt.

"So you want me to meet you at the police station?" Burns said.

"Hell no. If I go down there, I'll never get away. I'll have to read reports and sign 'em and listen to people bitch about one thing after another and God knows what all. This is supposed to be my day off."

"I'd think Saturday would be a big day for the police," Burns said.

"Look, Burns, I don't tell you how to teach Alfred, Lord Neuman—"

"Lord Tennyson."

"Whoever the hell. And you don't tell me how to run the police department."

"I wasn't trying to tell you—"

"I know what you wasn't trying to do. Anyhow, I'm not going down there till tonight. Saturday *night* is the busy time. Not during the day."

"I see. So do you want to come here?"

"Hell, no, I don't want to come there. Didn't I tell you this is my day off? I got things to do around the house. You come here."

"Come there?"

"For an English teacher you have a pretty tough time

with the King's English," Napier said. "Or maybe you just have a hearing problem."

"No, I heard you all right. You said for me to come there."

"You got it."

"Where is 'there'?" Burns asked.

Napier gave him the address. "You had lunch yet?"

As a matter of fact, Burns had not. It was the middle of the afternoon, but the events of the day had somehow pushed the thought of food from his consciousness.

"Me neither," Napier said. "Bring something when you come."

Burns was so surprised that for a second he couldn't think of anything to say. "What would you like?" he finally managed.

"Whatever. Just make it snappy." Napier hung up.

Burns stood and looked at the phone for a while. Then he got a move on. When Napier said make it snappy, he probably meant it.

Burns stopped by the Taco Bell drive-in window and picked up a bag of soft tacos, three for him and three for Napier. Then he located the address Napier had given him, which was right on the eastern edge of Pecan City, near the end of its main east/west street. The houses in that area were not new, and they were spread out, some of them sitting on two or three lots, with more acreage in the rear. More than one of them had a small barn in back, and Burns could see a horse in one of the barns.

Napier's house was set back from the road and surrounded by live oak trees that shaded the lawn of St. Augustine grass. The lawn was neatly clipped and still quite green, a neat trick in Pecan City, where the annual rainfall did not contribute much to the upkeep of a lawn. It was obvious that Napier's lawn had been carefully watered and fertilized, not to mention tenderly cared for.

Why that should have been a surprise, Burns wasn't quite sure, but it was. Not as big a surprise as being told to come to the house was, however. Burns wondered if maybe Napier had developed a liking for him.

He parked his car in the semicircular drive and got out. The house was small, probably two bedrooms, but like the yard it had been well taken care of.

On the door there was a brass knocker shaped like a cowboy boot. Burns banged the toe of the boot into the brass plate and waited.

Napier opened the door. He was wearing jeans and boots, and a white shirt that had small paint stains all over it—red, green, yellow, blue, black, gray. He was holding an artist's paint brush in his right hand. There was an odor of something in the air.

Turpentine? Burns wondered, standing in the doorway with the Taco Bell bag in his hand.

"Come on in, Burns," Napier said. "You look like hell with that bandage around your nose. What you got in the sack?"

"Soft tacos," Burns said, still trying to take in the sight of Napier with an artist's brush in his hand.

"Well don't just stand there till they get cold. Let's go back in the kitchen."

Burns followed the police chief through a short hall into a small den. They turned right into the kitchen/dining area, which was actually a part of the den.

That was when Burns got an even bigger surprise.

The table was set off in a small nook and partially covered with newspapers. On top of the newspapers were hundreds of tiny figures and numerous little bottles of paint. There were more brushes, too, like the one Napier had in his hand.

"Sit down, sit down," Napier said, taking the bag from Burns. "There's room. Just move the papers out of the way."

Burns sat in a wooden chair and looked at the figures on the table.

"Battle of Little Big Horn," Napier said. "Or it will be when I get 'em all painted."

Burns marveled at the detail of the tiny figures of cavalrymen and Indians, at the details of their dress, at the weapons they were carrying, at the poses they were striking. He marveled even more at the fine job Napier was doing with the painting. He was taking lifeless lumps of lead and making them into miniature works of art.

Napier sat in the chair opposite Burns, opened the bag, and looked inside. "You didn't bring any drinks," he said accusingly.

"I, uh, I forgot," Burns said, still looking at the figures. For some reason he found himself thinking of a student who had been in one of his classes many years before. The boy had seemed utterly hopeless. He could not spell his own name the same way twice, had no idea of the structure of an English sentence, and could no more organize a paper than he could circumnavigate the globe in an inner tube.

Burns had tried to get through to the boy, but it had been impossible. The boy just didn't seem to care, and Burns had finally given up, letting him drift along to take his failing grades with what appeared to be a complete lack of concern or desire to learn.

If anyone had asked him, Burns would have said the boy was hopeless, someone who should never have come to college in the first place and someone who certainly would never amount to anything, ever.

Then Burns had gone to a student art show. Walking around the room, he was struck by a group of paintings on one wall, paintings that at first looked like conventional portraits but which upon closer inspection showed a clarity of vision that even their subjects probably would never have suspected the artist possessed. Though he could never have said how it was done, Burns saw that the paintings revealed their subjects' personalities as clearly as anything Burns had ever seen. Looking at them, he felt as if he were looking right into the subjects' secret hearts. The effect was devastating.

And naturally they had been painted by the hopeless boy, whose barely legible signature Burns could make out in their lower right-hand corners.

Napier set a Pepsi in a twelve-ounce non-returnable bottle in front of Burns and sat back down. Burns had not even noticed that Napier had gotten up.

"You've done a really nice job on those soldiers," Burns said.

"I like to do it," Napier said around a mouthful of taco. "Relaxes me. I got a lot of stuff like that. Now tell me about those books."

Burns told him, but Napier wasn't satisfied.

"I know all that already. There must be more to it than that, or you wouldn't have wanted to talk to me." Napier took another taco from the bag and started in on it.

"Well, I was thinking that whoever defaced the books might be the same one who killed Street," Burns said.

"Defaced. You English teachers sure do talk good. But I'd already thought about that. What's more to the point is, why deface the books in the first place?"

Burns had an answer for that. He'd thought about it while he was waiting in the Emergency Room. "To show contempt for Street. If someone really wrote letters saying that Street wasn't the author of his own books, it must be someone who really hates the man."

"That reporter from Big D told me all about that letter, but he didn't show it to me." Napier rattled the bag as he brought out another taco. "You got any ideas about who wrote it?"

"None at all," Burns admitted, sipping the Pepsi.

"You just might be wasting my time, Burns," Napier said. "Why did whoever it was come back after the books, then?"

"Fingerprints," Burns said. He'd thought about that one.

"Jesus," Napier said. "You guys who read books are all alike. Do you know how likely it really is that we'd get a usable print off a book?"

"No," Burns said.

"Damn small, especially after you and Miss Scanner—"

"Tanner."

"—had put your own fingers all over it. And who knows who else besides. It'd been sitting on a library shelf, for God sake."

"If I didn't think about that, maybe the thief didn't think about it," Burns said.

Napier chewed thoughtfully. "You could be right. If he didn't think about fingerprints in the first place and wear gloves."

"We wouldn't be dealing with a professional," Burns said.

"I wish you hadn't said that," Napier told him.

"Said what?" Burns asked.

"'We,'" Napier said, going for another taco.

· 9 ·

On Monday, Burns got to his office early, as usual. He climbed the three flights of stairs with his usual alacrity, but he did not do anything about preparing the lecture for his first class. Instead, he sat in the chair at his desk and thought about his visit to Napier.

One thing that really aggravated Burns was that the police chief had eaten every single one of the tacos. All Burns got was the Pepsi.

And what had surprised Burns most was not the lead soldiers that Napier had been painting but what the chief had shown him just before Burns left: a whole room, intended by the builder as a small living room, devoted to miniature figures that filled the shelves on all four walls. There were Indians, farmers, cowboys, sports figures, Vikings, knights, bullfighters, spacemen, police, sailors, soldiers, and even a few dragons, all of them handpainted by Napier. And on the floor were models of the Alamo, Fort Apache, and the Roy Rogers Ranch.

"I got a set of Lincoln Logs, too," Napier said. "Still in the original box."

It wasn't that Burns didn't like Napier, it was simply that he liked thinking of him as Boss Napier, the man who relaxed by going into the forest with a bullwhip to subdue grizzly bears single-handedly. Thinking of him as someone who liked to paint tiny figures of spacemen and collect model toy sets three or four decades old made the man seem too human somehow.

And Napier was certainly human. As Burns was leaving, he said, "That Miss Tanager, she's single, right?"

"I believe she is," Burns said. "Why?"

"She's a good-looking woman, is all," Napier said, and Burns left him there in his paint-stained shirt. Hadn't Miss Tanner even said that Napier was a 'nice man'? It didn't bear thinking about.

On the positive side, Burns had learned a good deal about the questioning of the people in attendance at the seminar.

"Most of 'em are in the clear," Napier said. "They've all got alibis, except for the president, and the president of the school wouldn't kill anybody, would he?"

They had a good laugh over that one, and Burns never did get around to mentioning who had been the last person to check Street's books out of the library.

"I told 'em they could all go back where they came from," Napier said. "But that Dunkum, he's stayin' in town. This'll be big in all the papers, and I wouldn't be surprised to see a few of those TV folks in town."

Burns hadn't thought of that, but it just might turn out so that Miller got his national publicity. Somehow, Burns didn't think President Miller would be happy about it, however.

"Could Street have been killed by someone who just came to town, did the job, and left?" Burns asked.

"You talkin' about a professional hit?" Napier said. "No way."

"Well, he did write a book about the Bay of Pigs."

"I read it," Napier said, surprising Burns again. "I don't think he gave away any national secrets. I don't think the CIA sent out a hit man after him, not this many years after the book was published."

"Who do you think did it, then?"

"I don't know," Napier said. "You tell me."

Burns had no more idea than the chief did, but it seemed that Napier was almost asking him to get involved now, after having spent a lot of time and words warning him off. He said as much.

"You can take it any way you want to, Burns. But if you get in any trouble, it's your own look-out."

Burns had known that all along.

Burns got through his early class and went immediately to the History lounge to see how Tomlin and Fox had fared in the questioning. To his surprise, there was no one there.

He went to Fox's office, threading his way among the students who were changing classes. They were laughing and talking, exchanging friendly jibes and telling jokes, altogether a good bit more lively and cheerful than they had been only minutes before in the classroom.

Burns's two friends were standing in the doorway of the office, talking. Today Fox had on a pair of pants with green and white windowpane checks, a striped shirt, and a paisley tie that was about five inches wide.

Fox saw Burns headed toward them. "It's an outrage!" he said loudly, ignoring the curious glances of the students. "It's an absolute outrage. We're professional people. We don't have to put up with this kind of thing."

"What kind of thing?" Burns said when he reached them. "Did Boss Napier pistol-whip you?"

"Huh?" Fox said, a puzzled look on his face. "What are you talking about?"

"The same thing you are. About getting questioned by the police on Saturday."

"Oh," Fox said. "That. I'm not talking about that."

"It's worse than that," Tomlin said. "A lot worse."

"What, then?" Burns said. Most of the students had gone on by, finding their way to their next classrooms.

"We'll show you," Tomlin said, marching off in the direction of the History lounge. Fox fell in behind him, and Burns trailed along after them.

When they got there, Fox stepped in front of Tomlin and opened the door with a dramatic flourish. Burns looked inside.

"See?" Tomlin said.

The room looked the same as it had the last time Burns had been inside it, the same old table and chairs, the same cheesy shade on the light, the same ashtray on the table.

"I don't see anything," Burns said.

"On the wall," Fox told him. "Look on the wall."

The walls of the History lounge were nothing to brag about, being nothing but bare boards. There was no wallpaper, not even any sheetrock, to cover them.

There was, however, a small sign attached to the back wall, a sign that had not been there the previous Friday. It was made of black plastic and had white letters pressed into it. It said:

NO SMOKING
PUBLIC AREA

Fox was really fuming now. "Can you believe that? 'Public area,' my fat rump! When's the last time you ever saw any of the public in this place?"

"The public would probably be embarrassed to be caught dead in there, to tell the truth," Tomlin said.

"Who put the sign up?" Burns said.

Neither of the other men had thought about that, so Burns suggested that they ask Rose.

They found her in a storeroom located underneath the first floor stairs. The storeroom was small, and Rose took up most of it, since she was built something along the lines of a pro wrestler—a male pro wrestler—with powerful sloping shoulders and thick, muscular arms. She was smoking a cigarette.

"Rose," Burns said, "do you know anything about the sign in the History lounge?"

"Sho do," Rose said, blowing a thin stream of smoke out her nostrils, a skill Burns had often admired. When he had been a smoker, he had tried it once or twice. It burned his nose so much that he gave it up.

"Who put it there, then?" Fox demanded.

"I did," Rose said. "Mr. Fairly, he tole me to do it."

"Who told *him* to do it?" Fox asked.

"I didn' ax him that," Rose said. "He the boss, I jus' do what he say." She took another puff of her cigarette.

"He didn't tell you to put a sign in this room?" Tomlin asked.

Rose laughed. "He know better than that."

"I bet he does," Fox said. "All right, Rose. Thanks for telling us."

"Sho," Rose said.

The three men trooped glumly back upstairs to the lounge and sat around the table. Fox took out a pack of Cost Cutters and put it on the table. Then he began twirling it around.

"I thought you were never going to smoke those things," Burns said. "Didn't you tell me once that you thought the package was tacky?"

"Maybe," Fox said. "They're cheap though, and since the tax went up again, cheap is what I'm looking for, not style."

Burns tried to avoid looking at Fox's garage-sale clothes, but he couldn't help it. Tomlin was looking, too, and when he caught Burns's eye it was all they could do not to laugh.

"I bet it was Dorinda Edgely," Fox said. "She's the one who got them to put up that sign."

"Why would she do that?" Burns asked. He had been doing very well without smoking, but he found that the sign made him want to light up and to keep on lighting up. He hadn't wanted a cigarette in days, hadn't even really thought about one, but the damned sign was working on him. In reverse.

"She's poked her head in here once or twice," Fox said. "And she saw you two smoking. She's just the kind who'd try to get it stopped."

Fox was right, Burns thought, not that it really mattered who got the sign put there. The sign *was* there, and there was actually a state law banning smoking in public areas. So there was nothing they could do about it, short of complaining to the president, and they were not about to do that.

Burns turned the subject to the murder and the questioning.

"Nothing to it," Tomlin said. "I was at home with Joynell when it happened. The coppers can't pin a thing on me."

Tomlin avoided looking at Burns when he talked, but there was nothing unusual in that; it was just a part of Tomlin's nature. Several of his students had once told Burns that Tomlin, though he taught Education and often talked of the value of looking at the audience, never once made eye contact with them in his classes. His gaze always seemed to be directed just above their heads. They often wondered what he was looking at and concluded it was the row of portraits of great educators—men like Socrates, Rousseau, Dewey, and Piaget—that lined the back wall of the classroom. So one day they went to class early and took the portraits down, laying them on the floor in the back of the room. Tomlin never even noticed. He lectured the class as usual, looking somewhere above their heads the entire time. The students put the pictures back up and left just as puzzled as ever.

"They can't pin anything on me either," Fox said. "Loretta and I were watching TV most of the night, and then Mal picked me up to go to the seminar in the morning."

Burns hadn't really suspected them of any part in the murder. "I was just wondering about the questioning," he said. "Did Boss Napier give you a hard time?"

"Sure he did," Tomlin answered. "What would you expect? Called me a wimp college teacher and told me he was going to put me in a cell with a gorilla if I lied to him. Not a gorilla like a tough guy. A real gorilla."

"Told me the same thing," Fox said. "But I didn't let it bother me." He glared at the sign. "Now *that* bothers me."

"Not me," Tomlin said suddenly. He reached into his shirt pocket and took out his pack of Merits. He shook one out, got his lighter out of his pocket, and lit up. He sat there puffing contentedly as Fox and Burns stared at him.

"Aren't you worried that they'll get you?" Fox said. He was always worried that he would be caught smoking, but now that there was an official sign he was doubly worried.

"Hell, no," Tomlin told him. "Like you said, who ever comes in here? Rose might, but she'll never tell. If Dorinda Edgely catches me, let her run tattle to the president. I'll deny it, and you two can back me up. It'll be our word against hers."

"Well, . . ." Fox said.

"Besides," Tomlin said, "we can make Burns sit with his chair against the door. If he's not going to smoke, he might as well be useful."

That settled it. Burns moved his chair and soon Fox was happily blowing smoke rings, or trying to. Things were back to normal. It was almost as if Street had never been killed.

And then they started in on Burns about his nose.

At lunch that day, Burns went to talk to Clem Nelson. She was in her office, eating an apple and a bran muffin. Burns, who had seen a story on *60 Minutes* about a possible carcinogen that was often sprayed on apples, tried to convince her that eating one was probably almost as bad as smoking, but she didn't pay him any mind.

Then he asked about her questioning by Napier.

"He was a perfect gentleman," Clem said, wrapping the apple core in her napkin before throwing it away.

A sexist, Burns thought. He talked tough to the men and came on like a charmer to the women. It figured.

He told Clem about the letter Duncan claimed to have received and how it appeared to be accusing Street of either theft or plagiarism.

"I don't believe that Edward Street would do such a thing," Clem said. "It's true that there were times when he might not have gotten along with the rest of us because he had such an exaggerated sense of his own importance, but he would never steal."

"I've often wondered, though, why he never wrote another novel," Burns said.

Clem looked away and fumbled with a red pencil that was lying on top of her blonde-wood desk. That wasn't like Clem, who always looked directly at Burns when she was speaking to him, unlike Mal Tomlin.

"Is there something you ought to be telling me?" Burns asked her.

"Maybe," Clem said, still looking at the pencil.

Burns waited.

Clem put the pencil in a gold and black HGC Panthers coffee mug that she used for a pencil holder. Then she took it out again and bounced its eraser end on top of the desk.

"All right," she said finally. "I'll tell you. I think Street *had* written another book."

Burns had suspected that she knew something, but not something like that. "How do you know?" he said.

"He wrote me a letter," Clem said, looking at the pencil.

"Did you mention this to Boss Napier?" Burns asked.

"No. He didn't give me a chance. He just asked about my whereabouts on the night Street was killed and whether I knew anyone who had a grudge against him."

"Did you?" Burns said. "Know anyone who had a grudge against him, I mean?"

"Well, not really. Nothing that anyone would kill for, at least."

Burns remembered his experiences of the previous year. "You can't be sure about that," he said. "But tell me about the letter."

"It was addressed to me here at the school," Clem said.

She put down the pencil and opened the top drawer of her desk. "Here it is" She brought out a piece of plain white paper with typing on it.

She handed it to Burns, who saw at once that the sides of the paper were not quite smooth, as if perforated edges had been torn off.

"Printer paper," Burns said. He read the letter.

Dear Clem,
I know you're looking forward to seeing me again. I've been quite a success since my days at HGC, but I've never really forgotten you or all the others I knew in my teaching days there. In fact, I think about all of you quite often, so often that I've been working on a new book that is set in a college much like HGC. I'm sure that many of you will be wondering whether you appear in the story, but don't worry. The book will be a pure work of fiction. I would never reveal any of the things I learned about the inner workings of HGC during my tenure there. No one would believe it if I did. I do think the book will be a big seller and add to my already established reputation. I hope you'll buy a copy on publication. I know you'll enjoy it.

The letter was signed "sincerely" by Street.

"Pretty strange letter, don't you think?" Burns said.

"I told you that Street was something of a blowhard, didn't I?" Clem said.

"I found that out for myself. But that's not what I meant."

"I don't see anything strange about it aside from that," Clem said. "It sounds typical of Street, the way I remember him."

"Read it again," Burns suggested, "It's addressed to you, but it could just as well have been addressed to anyone. I'll bet he sent a copy of this to everyone he knew from his teaching days here."

Clem looked over the letter. "You could be right," she said. "I wondered why he singled me out."

"Another thing," Burns said. "It sounds almost like a threat to me."

"He's protesting too much, you mean. Yes, I saw that when I read it the first time."

"Right. 'I would never reveal any of the things I know.' Or, 'No one would believe it if I did.' Sounds to me as if he might have been indirectly threatening to let the world know about things that happened here, whatever those things were."

"Nothing ever happens here," Clem said.

"You've got to be kidding," Burns said.

Clem smiled. "I guess I am."

"I wish you'd told me about this letter before the seminar."

"I only got it the other day," Clem said. "The day school began. I didn't tell you because I thought you might worry unnecessarily."

"I would have worried, all right," Burns said. *But not unnecessarily,* he thought.

When Burns went back to his office, he noticed something lying on the wide stone ledge outside the north window of his office.

He walked around his desk for a closer look.

It was a dead pigeon.

·10·

Burns spent the better part of an hour worrying about the dead pigeon. He couldn't imagine why there would be a dead bird on the window ledge. Bunni came by to ask about the murder, and she was horrified. She didn't like live birds, much less dead ones, and she did not even stay to talk. Her fascination with the murder and with Burns's nose was less than her disgust at the sight of the bird. She went back to her desk near the offices of Larry and the Darryls.

Then Burns had a visitor. Harold Duncan stood in the doorway of the office, or rather he leaned there. His chest was heaving, and it was obvious that he had suffered greatly from his climb up the three impressive flights of stairs to Main's top floor. He didn't say anything for a full minute, just stood there and panted while Burns looked at him.

"You should have them move you to a lower floor," Duncan said when he finally caught his breath.

"I like it here," Burns said. "I'm usually safe from the administration." *And other unwanted visitors*, he didn't add.

"Yeah, I'll bet, and you're not easy to find even when a

guy gets the stairs climbed," Duncan said. "You got a minute?"

Burns didn't particularly want to talk to the reporter, but he thought he might as well. "Sure. Have a seat."

Duncan entered the office. The dead pigeon caught his eye at once. "You ought to have something done about that. I'll bet it's diseased."

Psittacosis. Burns hadn't thought of that, until now.

"I'll call someone," he said, wondering how he was going to explain to Clarice Bond about the dead bird. "What can I do for you, Mr. Duncan?"

The reporter ran the fingers of his right hand through his thin hair and looked around the office. "You got an ashtray in here?"

Burns got a Mr. Pibb can out of the trash. "You can use this."

"You sure you don't mind?" Duncan said. "Lots of people these days don't want me smoking in their offices."

Burns was sure that not many people welcomed Duncan into their offices whether he smoked or not. He was an unsavory-looking character, and Burns suspected that the newspaper didn't send him out on the bigger assignments. If the editor had known beforehand that Street would be killed, Duncan would still be in Dallas.

"Go ahead," Burns said. "Smoking doesn't bother me."

"Good," Duncan said. He was wearing an old linen sports coat and he took a pack of Camel Filters from the inside pocket. After he got one lit he took a small spiral notebook and a ballpoint pen from the same pocket. He flipped the notebook open and said, "Looks like you had a little trouble. Want to tell me about it?"

"No," Burns said.

"That's all right. What's your opinion of the murder of Edward Street?"

"I think it's a real shame," Burns said. "Edward Street was a talented writer, and our seminar was only the beginning of the academic and critical recognition that was bound to come his way sooner or later. And for him to—"

"What a crock," Duncan said. "I wasn't expecting you to toe the party line, Burns."

Burns wondered irrelevantly how Duncan would have spelled "toe." All Burns's students were beginning to spell it "tow," as in "tow the line."

"I didn't mean to be giving you anything but what you asked for," Burns said.

"What I was asking for was an opinion about who killed the man," Duncan said.

"How about you? He called you a little slug and threatened to stomp you, didn't he?" Burns really didn't like Duncan much. Maybe it was the way he looked.

Duncan shrugged. "I get that kind of thing all the time. Doesn't bother me."

"Was there really a letter claiming that Street didn't write those books?" Burns asked.

"Sure there was. I wouldn't make something like that up. I'm a legitimate reporter, not a gossip-monger." Duncan crushed out his cigarette on top of the soda can and stuck the butt inside.

"Maybe the murderer wrote that letter," Burns said. "I'd like to see it."

"Well, you can't. The cops took it. Came by my room Saturday and got it. Said it was evidence in the case."

So much for that idea, Burns thought, somewhat surprised that Duncan had given in to the request of the Pecan City police. He thought reporters were supposed to be tougher than that.

"What did the letter say?" he asked.

"Just what I said it did. That Street didn't write the books."

"It didn't say who did write them?"

"Not even a hint."

Burns was about to ask if Duncan had any ideas on the subject when he saw someone walking down the short hallway to his office. It was Melinda Land, the professor from Houston. Burns was surprised to see her there. He thought

• 92 •

that everyone who attended the seminar would have gone back to their respective universities by now.

"Hello, Dr. Burns," she said when she got to the door. "Mr. Duncan." She did not seem winded at all and was clearly in better shape than Duncan. *In more ways than one,* Burns thought admiringly.

Burns stood up, as he always did when pretty redheads walked into his office. "Hello, Dr. Land. I thought you'd be back in Houston by now." He pulled the chair from under the typing table and placed it where she could sit in it.

She sat gracefully and smiled at him. "No. I just couldn't go back, not with all the excitement here. I've always been an admirer of Edward Street's works, and I saw this as a good opportunity to do a little writing of my own, sort of the ironic story of how a man returns in triumph to the little school where he began his career and dies a terrible death."

"Sounds like a sob sister bit to me," Duncan said. He had not moved from his seat. "You should leave that to us professionals."

He seemed to Burns to have the usual reporter's disdain for academic types. For that matter, Street had shared that disdain, though he had once been a professor himself. It was strange how writers usually looked down on those who devoted themselves to the study of writing and writers.

"I can assure you that I will do a professional job," Dr. Land said. Her tone was icy.

"Well, just don't ask for any help from me," Duncan said.

"You don't have to worry on that account," Dr. Land assured him. "I'd like to talk to you sometime when you have a free moment, Dr. Burns. About Street's years here at HGC, his friends, things like that."

"Wait a minute," Duncan said. "I was here first. I was asking about that stuff." He hadn't been, but that didn't seem to bother him. He was probably working on the biggest story of his career, and he didn't want any competition, Burns thought.

Burns held up a hand. "As much as I'd like to talk to both of you, I can't really help you. I wasn't here when Street taught here. You'd better talk to Miss Nelson."

"Who's she?" Duncan said.

Burns, hating himself, though not as much as Clem would, told him.

Burns escaped to the library after Duncan and Dr. Land left. He often escaped there, into the stacks to read old magazines or into the periodicals room to read new ones.

This time, however, he had an entirely different destination in mind—Miss Tanner's office. He had never visited her before, but the events of Saturday seemed to offer him a perfectly good excuse.

He smiled at the student worker behind the check-out desk and walked on back of the elevator to the librarian's office. The door was closed.

Burns tapped on the door.

"Come in," Miss Tanner said, her voice muffled by the door, which was considerably thicker than the hollow-core door to Burns's own office.

He opened the door and went in. Miss Tanner looked up at him as she closed the bottom drawer of her desk.

"Oh, hello, Carl," she said.

"Hello, Elaine," he said, trying to be casual about the use of her first name. He knew that nowadays everyone used first names, but it had always irritated him. Let an insurance salesman inside your house, and within two seconds he would have called you by your first name five times. Burns couldn't operate like that. He usually had to know a person quite well before venturing into first-name territory.

"You almost caught me in the act," Elaine said with a sheepish laugh.

"Doing what?" Burns asked. He looked around the office. What would a pretty woman have been doing behind a locked library door? Everything seemed perfectly normal.

"Doing this," she said. She opened the desk drawer and

brought out a pink plastic bottle. "Blowing bubbles. Close the door, please."

Burns closed the door, wondering if he had heard her correctly. Blowing bubbles?

The bottle had a yellow cap, which Elaine removed. She stuck her fingers, which Burns noticed had red-painted nails, inside the bottle and pulled out a pink plastic bar with circles on each end. Puckering her lips, she blew through one end, producing a cloud of transparent bubbles, all of them reflecting the fluorescent lights from the ceiling.

One of the bubbles hit Burns on the tip of the nose and burst.

"I hope that didn't hurt," Elaine said.

"No," Burns said. He was beginning to wonder about Elaine. First the trophies, now the bubbles. HGC had a way of attracting the eccentrics, but he had hoped Elaine would not be one of them.

"I do this when I get frustrated," she explained. "It helps relieve the tension."

"I see," Burns said. "What was the problem?"

"It was that reporter, Duncan." She blew another bunch of bubbles that floated around the office. "He came by and asked all kinds of questions."

"Did you tell him about Saturday?" Burns said.

"Yes, he got it out of me. I didn't intend to, but somehow I did." She blew more bubbles.

Burns liked looking at her lips as she pursed them to blow. Now he understood why Duncan hadn't pursued the question about his nose. He already knew the answer. Duncan was probably smarter than Burns had thought. It didn't do to underestimate anyone. Burns thought again of the student who had been so poor in English and so good in art.

"How long do you have to wear that bandage?" Elaine asked. She capped the bubble bottle and put it back in the drawer.

"Not too long," Burns said. "I know it looks kind of funny, but—"

"I don't think it looks funny. I think it's cute."

Burns grinned foolishly. "I was wondering," he said. "We have a home game this coming Saturday, and I thought maybe you'd like to go." He had no idea what made him say it. He certainly had not intended to, or he didn't think he had. It was too late to take it back, however.

"Of course I would," Elaine said. "I don't know much about football, but I think we should support the college teams."

"Right," Burns said. "Absolutely." Knowing about football wasn't really necessary for watching HGC's team, anyway. In fact, the less you knew, the more you could enjoy the game. "I'll pick you up about one o'clock."

"All right. I hope that nasty reporter won't be around by then."

"What did he say that got you so upset?" Burns asked.

"All kinds of things. He said that he had looked for me on Saturday, but that he missed me because I got out of the building so fast after my interview with Mr. Napier. I told him that I had to meet you, and then he made a snide remark. So I had to tell him that it was strictly business, and then I had to explain what I meant. So he found out everything."

"I don't suppose it matters," Burns said. "The way my nose looks, I can't keep telling people I bumped into a door." That was exactly what he had told Tomlin and Fox, not that they had believed him.

"It's all such a mess," Elaine said. "I just wish Mr. Napier could find out who killed Street and it would all be over."

Burns felt the same way, but he didn't have as much faith in 'Mr. Napier' as Elaine did. And he didn't like the soft way she said his name, either. It wasn't easy for a sedentary English teacher to compete with a man of action.

"I'm sure it will all be over by Saturday," he said, hoping that he was not being overly optimistic.

"It had better be," Elaine said. As Burns left her office, she was getting the bubble maker out of the desk drawer again.

As usual in Texas in early September, the weather was still quite warm. Burns noticed that the grass around Main was drying, except where it was shaded by the tall pecan trees, and he wondered if there was a new economy drive on to save water. There had been a time, right after he first arrived at HGC, that the lawn was something to brag about. That was because Dr. Rogers, the president at that time and not then under the influence of Dean Elmore, had taken a great deal of pride in the school's appearance.

Every spring was heralded, if that was the right word, by the smell that filled the air, the smell of dried sheep shit. Rogers had it brought in by the truckload and dumped on the campus, after which the custodial staff could be seen for days raking and smoothing and covering the grass with the odorous manure. The smell pervaded everywhere, the courtyards, the classrooms, and even the cafeteria. But the lawn was always lush and green. The fact that it was frequently watered during the summer months helped, too.

The shade of the pecan trees felt cool as Burns walked under them. Most of them were far taller than Main's three stories, and in years when conditions were right they produced a good crop of pecans. Mal Tomlin was especially fond of the nuts and could often be seen strolling the campus, picking up handfuls of pecans. He cracked them and ate them in his office and in the history lounge, the floor of which was sometimes covered with their hulls.

Burns entered the building and cantered up the stairs to the third floor. Clem was still in her office, grading papers, so he stopped by for a minute.

"Did the reporter and Dr. Land find you?" he asked.

"Yes," Clem said, putting down her red pen. "And you can wipe that innocent look off your face. I know who sent them."

"I wouldn't exactly say I sent them," Burns protested, though not very strongly.

"I would," Clem said.

"I'm sorry," Burns said. Then, "I was wondering if you could tell me what you told them."

"Word for word?"

"Maybe not. Just who the faculty members are who might have gotten letters like yours from Street, the ones who were here when he taught at HGC."

"I can tell you that easily enough," Clem said. "There's Miss Darling, for one. Abner Swan, Don Elliott, Mary Winsor, and Dick Hayes. Most of the others have either retired or gone on to other jobs by now."

Hayes was the chairman of the Department of Business, and Mary Winsor *was* the journalism department. She taught all the courses, supervised the school paper and yearbook, and even wrote a great many of the school's press releases.

"What about Mr. Fairly?" Burns said.

Clem thought for a second, twirling the red pen in her fingers. "I hadn't considered him," she admitted. "I suppose I have a habit of thinking about the faculty and not the members of the maintenance staff. But Mr. Fairly was here then."

"He must have been pretty young," Burns said.

"He was. It was his first job, I believe. He couldn't have been more than nineteen or twenty. He didn't go to college, of course. He had been working for a lawn care service or something of that sort, and the owner went bankrupt. He came here, and he's been here ever since."

"He's moved up in the world, though," Burns said. "He's head of the whole shebang now."

"That's true. And of course he knew Street."

Burns thought again about the rifle.

"That's what I was afraid of," he said.

Burns went back to his office, intending to make a little list. He did not do so immediately, however. He could only stand in the office doorway and survey the damage.

It wasn't anyone's fault, really, except his own. He knew

that. It was a character flaw that he had tried to correct but never could: he kept a really messy desk.

He didn't know why. It wasn't that he liked clutter, and in fact he often expressed admiration of the desks in the offices of his colleagues. They often had large areas of cleared space where the top of the desk could actually be seen, and the papers that were in sight were neatly stacked in what appeared to Burns's wondering eyes to be organized and orderly piles.

Burns's desktop was organized, too, but he was the only one who understood the organization. There were graded papers there, and papers yet to be graded. There were memos to be replied to and letters to be answered. There were textbooks to be read, and there were notes for his different classes.

These things were not necessarily in orderly stacks, however, and the system drove Rose crazy. She liked to do her job and to do it right, and she believed that her job included dusting the office furniture. In every office. Including Burns's office.

She managed to restrain herself most of the time, but every so often, say once a month or so, she could stand it no longer and she dusted Burns's desk. To do so, she had to move everything on it, and she could never put it back exactly where it should have been. It usually took him a couple of days to set things right.

Obviously, Rose had been in while he was gone. The desktop was neater than he ever left it, the papers all in stacks, the letters neatly arranged, the memos separated from the letters. Burns knew that he should have simply said something to Rose, but he didn't have the nerve.

Still, there was something that was not quite right about the neatness. It was not exactly Rose's kind of neatness.

Burns never locked his office door; he never even closed it until he left in the afternoon. It would have been easy for anyone to walk in and go through everything there.

Maybe he was wrong. He would ask Rose later. Right now, he wanted to make his list.

It wasn't very long. It contained only names: Clem Nelson, Miss Darling, Abner Swan, Mary Winsor, Dick Hayes, and Don Elliott. Mr. Fairly's name was on it, too, but there was a question mark after it. Burns doubted that Street had even known Fairly. He would find out, though. He was going to talk to the people on the list. No matter what Napier might think about his doing so.

He looked out the window. The pigeon was still on the ledge, so he reluctantly picked up the phone to call Clarice Bond.

·11·

Burns had no sooner hung up from his singularly uncommunicative conversation with Clarice about the pigeon than the phone rang, startling him. By that time of the afternoon, Main was virtually deserted, and he rarely got any calls after one o'clock. He was sure that it couldn't be good news.

He was right. It was Miller's secretary, informing him that Miller wanted to talk to him. In person. At once.

Burns sighed and hung up.

The HGC administration was currently ensconced in an old warehouse, where their offices had been moved after the fire that destroyed the former Administration Building the previous year. Most of the warehouse was given over to the maintenance crew, and Burns caught a glimpse of Mr. Fairly sitting at his desk and discussing something with Clarice Bond.

Dead pigeons, probably, Burns thought, and then wondered what kind of discussion anyone could have with Clarice.

Miller's office was at the back of the warehouse, and like all the others had his name written on a white card taped to the door. Burns thought that the administrators should have plastic signs made, like the one in the History lounge, but the offices were supposed to be merely temporary.

He tapped on the door and entered. Miller's secretary, who had replaced the former president's, was a rather severe young woman. Burns thought of her as looking something like Marilyn Quayle.

"Dr. Miller is expecting you," she said, and Burns went on past her and into the president's inner sanctum.

Whereas Dr. Rogers's office in the Administration Building had been decorated with pictures of Rogers shaking hands with famous men and women, Dr. Miller had his own style. The walls of his office had recently been paneled with a light-toned wood, but they were not hung with pictures. His diplomas were there, however, along with all kinds of other framed documents informing whoever was interested that Miller was an Outstanding Educator of the South, and Outstanding Young Man of America, and a member in good standing of the Rotary Club. He had honorary degrees from two universities, and he had received an honorable discharge from the United States Army.

Against one wall there was a bookcase filled with volumes of history, the discipline Miller had studied as an undergraduate and graduate student. Burns thought he caught a glimpse of Street's books sandwiched in among studies of the Gilded Age and the robber barons.

Miller was sitting at his desk writing something on the school's letterhead. He looked up at Burns.

"This business with Street is not good for the school from a public relations standpoint," the president said. "I can't imagine what could be worse."

Burns could. Elmore had been worse, for example, even before he died, and of course his murder had generated a bit of unwanted publicity. But that had been mostly local; the story had a brief play in the papers around the state and then died down. The murder of a best-selling writer, however, was another story.

"We're going to be on the *CBS Evening News,*" Miller said. "Your seminar has really gotten us in a mess."

Burns wanted to scream *"My* seminar?" at the top of his lungs, but he knew better than to do it. He didn't say anything, just stood there and looked at Miller.

"Sit down, sit down," Miller said.

Burns sat in a worn armchair that looked as if it had come from one of Fox's garage sales. It didn't seem to sit level, but that might have been because of the floor.

"Something's got to be done," Miller said. "And you've got to do it."

"The police chief warned me to stay out of it," Burns said, though he knew that wasn't strictly true. He didn't even know exactly why he said it, since both Miller—and Napier in his own way—seemed to be asking him to do exactly what he really wanted to do, namely, to snoop around. He didn't want to have any actual responsibility, however. Maybe that was why he was hesitant to commit himself.

"The police chief doesn't run this school," Miller said. "It's not his a—his rear-end that's on the line. You've done this kind of thing before, as I understand it."

"That was more or less an accident," Burns said truthfully, wondering who had been tattling to Miller. He had enjoyed playing his part in the investigation of Elmore's murder, however. Probably he had read too much Ross Macdonald.

"I don't give a hoot in he—hoot whether it was an accident or not," Miller said. His face was getting red, and Burns wondered if the poor man had a heart condition or suffered from high blood pressure. "I want you to get to the bottom of this, Burns. You can be sure that everyone on campus will cooperate with you. The sooner this is over and forgotten, the better."

Burns wanted to say he'd love to do it, but still he hesitated. It wasn't the danger. He already had a broken nose, after all.

"I'm not sure I want to pry in the personal lives of my friends," he said.

"Well, you'd better want to," Miller said. "English teachers are a dime a dozen, Burns."

There it was, the barely veiled threat. Burns had hoped that Miller would be above that sort of thing. Even Elmore, whom Burns had detested, would never have stooped to indirect threats. No, Elmore had always been much more direct.

"Naturally, I'll be glad to ask a few questions, if you think it's for the good of the school," Burns said.

"That's better," Miller said, some of the redness fading from his face. "I'll expect you to report your findings directly to me. Keep me posted every day. More often than that if you find anything out. And if anyone refuses to cooperate, just let me know."

"What about Boss Napier?" Burns asked.

"I told you, Burns, Napier does not run this college. Our duty is first to HGC and then to the community."

Burns wondered what Street would think about that. He said, "I'll have to let Napier know if I find anything out. I believe he would insist on it."

"You tell me first," Miller said. His Chamber of Commerce demeanor was not holding up well in his first big crisis.

"All right," Burns said, crossing his fingers. He would much rather cross his fingers than to cross Boss Napier. Napier might play with toy soldiers, but Burns had still not ruled out the bullwhip.

"Fine," Miller said. "I'm glad we've come to an understanding." He turned back to the letter he had been writing.

Burns got up to go and shot another quick look at the bookcase. Street's books were there, all right, and Burns was certain that he could see on the bottom of the spine the spots where the library's call numbers had once been stuck.

Burns's car was parked on the street in front of Main, so he walked back toward the building. It was too late to go back to the office, and he did not have any papers to grade, so he decided to go on home. Catch the *CBS Evening News*.

He thought about the two books he had seen on Miller's

shelves. It was possible that he could be wrong. It was hard to be certain from a distance that the spines were marred, but he would have given a pretty penny to see the pages of the books. If the books were indeed the ones that had until recently been in the HGC library, Miller was trying the old "Purloined Letter" gambit, but it wasn't going to work, not with keen-eyed private eye Carl Burns on the case.

And that is precisely what I am, Burns thought. A private eye, although not in possession of a license, engaged by the school's president to solve a crime.

Burns enjoyed mystery novels, particularly the stories of Lew Archer and Philip Marlowe and Nero Wolfe. He had sometimes in his private fantasies pictured himself as Archie Goodwin reporting to Wolfe as the great man lay in bed, his one-seventh of a ton reclining in yellow pajamas. But he had never really thought he would find himself to be an actual investigator. In the case of Elmore's death, he had been regarded by Napier as more of a nuisance than anything else, though Burns, not Napier, had been the one to come up with the solution.

He realized that he was also in a position of dubious legality, but so long as he did no more than snoop around the campus, Napier probably wouldn't care. He had seemed to be asking for some help himself. Perhaps he had recognized Burns's great investigative skills and—

Burns shut down that line of thought. No need to get carried away. He had gotten lucky once, and he had almost gotten himself killed in the bargain. This time, he was going to watch his step.

His path to Main took him by the Journalism Building, which Burns suspected had once been an Army barracks. At least that was what it looked like, a long wooden building painted white, with the words "JOURNALISM, HGC," painted on the side. Beneath them there was a drawing of something that was supposed to represent a panther but that looked to Burns a lot more like a domestic house cat with long fangs.

Burns knew that of all the faculty members, Mary Winsor put in the longest hours. She was probably still in her office. If he was going to play private eye, he might as well get started.

He mounted the wooden steps, shaded by an enormous old elm tree, and entered the building. The barracks, if that was what it had been, was now divided into several parts. At one end, to Burns's left, was Mary's office. To his right were two more offices, much smaller ones, and a classroom. There was also a classroom behind the wall in front of him. That was the room where the journalism students, what few of them there were, put the school's publications together.

There wasn't much going on since it was a Monday and the school paper did not appear until Friday. In fact, there were no students in sight. But the door to Mary's office was open, so Burns walked in.

The office was quite large. Besides Mary's desk it contained two bookshelves, a wicker sofa and two wicker chairs, and stacks of old yearbooks and newspapers. There was even a pallid bust of Pallas, on a water-stained wooden stand. Or maybe it was Diana or Hera for all Burns knew. The wicker furniture was old. The cushions were faded and the paint was peeling off the wickerwork. There were colorful afghans that Mary had knitted herself tossed on the backs of the chairs and the sofa. She probably owned the furniture, just as Clem probably owned hers.

Mary was behind the desk. She was a small woman who always looked harried. Her clothes never fit her quite right, and her hair was never under complete control. There was always a stray curl or sprig of gray sticking up in the air or out to the side. She was the kind of woman things happened to.

There were just people like that, Burns thought, and Mary happened to be one of them. She got all the strange students, for one thing.

There were other things, too. Last year her grandchildren had come for a visit and she had taken them to the park. Driving home they had seen a turtle in the road. The tender-hearted grandchildren had wanted to save the turtle, which they were convinced would soon be squashed to a bloody pulp if they left it there. Mary, equally tender-hearted, agreed with them and stopped to let them carry it to the side of the road.

The turtle, an old mossback, did not see things their way. He did not want to be saved or even bothered. He bit Mary's grandson on the hand, nipping the end off one finger. How many people could say their grandchildren had been bitten by a turtle?

And of course the kid had to have a tetanus shot, besides losing the tip of his finger.

And then, while Mary waited in the Emergency Room with the boy, her car was stolen.

And two weeks later, in a freak hailstorm, the roof of her house was ruined. Her husband, an absent-minded gentleman, had failed to mail in the home insurance payment the previous quarter.

And then . . . but Burns didn't want to think of anything else. He was sure Mary would have something new to tell him.

She looked up and saw him in the doorway. "Come in, Carl. This is a nice surprise. What on earth happened to your nose?"

Burns walked in and sat on the sofa. It was just as uncomfortable as it looked. "It was an accident," he said. He leaned back on the sofa, but a stray piece of wicker concealed in the afghan poked him in the small of the back. He sat up.

"How are things going, Mary?" he asked. With Mary, that was always enough of an opening.

"Oh, dear," she said. "Do you mind if I shut the door?"

"I'll get it," Burns said. He got up and closed the door. He knew he was in for a good story. Mary liked to tell the racier stories in private.

After Burns returned to his seat, Mary named a student. "Have you ever taught him?" she asked.

Burns had not.

"He's a ministerial student," Mary said. "He's taking my mass media course for some reason. It's at eight o'clock, you know."

Burns didn't know, but he nodded as if he did.

"Well," Mary went on, "I don't believe he's been on time for a single class this year. Of course, we've only been in school a short time, but I believe in promptness. Don't you?"

Burns agreed that he did.

"So this morning I asked him why he was always late, and he told me." Miss Winsor looked around the office as if she suspected that someone might be hiding behind a chair. "Do you know what he said?"

Burns had to admit that he did not.

"He said that he and his wife were trying to have a baby. And that the only time she was in the mood was early in the morning." Mary blushed furiously and shook her head. "Can you imagine saying a thing like that? To your teacher? In front of the whole class?"

Burns could not. When he had been in school, teachers were respected and, if the truth be known, feared. He would no more have confessed something like that to one of his college professors than he would have mooned one of his classes during the final exam, though he didn't put it like that to Mary.

"I don't know why those things happen to me," she said.

Burns didn't know either, and although it was an interesting subject, it was time to get down to cases. "I'd like to talk to you about Edward Street," he said.

"Poor Edward," Mary said. It seemed to Burns that she might be blushing, but maybe she was still thinking about her outspoken student. "He wasn't really so bad."

"I was wondering about enemies that he might have had, someone who was holding a grudge against him. You didn't happen to get a letter from him recently, by any chance?"

How's that for slipping one in casually? Burns thought.

Mary was taken aback. "How did you know about that?"

"It was just a guess," Burns said, pleased with himself. "I know of someone else who did. I wonder if you got the same letter."

"The one I received said that Edward had written another book, and that this one would have a college setting," Mary said.

"That's the same one. Do you know whether Street knew anything damaging about anyone who still teaches here at HGC?"

Mary ducked her head in confusion. There was no question about it. She was blushing because of the questions about Street, not because of anything her student had said.

"I imagine he knew a lot of things," she said.

Burns felt like a hotshot detective. He'd pushed the right buttons from the very first. "For example?" he said.

"Nothing in particular," Mary said quickly. "I just meant that anyone who teaches here naturally hears all kinds of things."

That was the truth, as Burns well knew, but he did not believe that was what Mary had meant at first.

"There must have been something specific on your mind," he said. "Did he know something about Dick Hayes? Or maybe Don Elliott?"

"Why Dick Hayes?"

"No reason. He just happens to have been here since Street's day. That's all."

"Oh. Well, there is that story about Dick and the student."

"The one he married?" Burns asked. He had heard the story, and it was unique only in the respect that Hayes had gotten away with it. In Burns's years at HGC, student/faculty relationships, in the intimate sense of the word, had been the cause for dismissal of more than one faculty member, including one member of the religion faculty. "What's strange about that?"

"Nothing," Mary said. "His wife was dying, after all, and he was certainly discreet if he was dating the girl. She did work in his office, but as far as I know, no one ever saw them together until after his wife had died."

"And they waited a year after that to get married," Burns said, repeating what he had heard. "What does that have to do with Street?"

"I think poor Edward was interested in that girl. There was a rumor around campus that Dick had in some way sped up the death of his wife, and Dick believed Edward had started it. There was quite a fuss about it, and some kind of confrontation. I don't recall how it all turned out, though."

Great, Burns thought. This is just the kind of stuff I need. He was hoping that Clem would remember the episode if he jogged her memory. And of course he would talk to Hayes about it.

"Can you remember anything else like that, any old grudges, arguments, anything at all?"

"No," she said. "Nothing."

Somehow Burns got the feeling that she was holding back on him. But that was all right. He felt that he had done a great job so far, and he just knew that he would do as well or better with his next victim. Or subject. Or whatever private eyes called the people they interviewed. He didn't remember Lew Archer ever saying exactly.

He stood up. "It's been nice talking to you, Mary. I hope your student and his wife get their wish soon."

"They'd better," Mary said. "One more tardy and I'm going to dismiss him from the class."

·12·

Leaving the Journalism Building, Burns bumped into Melinda Land. Literally. He was thinking about what he had learned from Mary Winsor, and he wasn't watching where he was going.

Melinda Land was soft and resilient. Burns didn't mind bumping into her at all.

"Excuse me," he said. "I didn't mean—"

"That's all right," Melinda said. "I was preoccupied myself. I should have been watching."

Burns smiled. "Working on your story?"

"Yes. I'm going to talk to Mrs. Winsor. Is she in her office?"

"Yes," Burns said. It hadn't occurred to him that he was going to be crossing paths with Melinda and with Duncan again so soon, but of course they would be talking to the same people he would be. "Did you and Duncan divide up the work?"

Melinda wrinkled her nose as if she smelled something bad. "He's a vile little man," she said. "I suppose he must be a good reporter, but he doesn't know much about people."

"Why do you say that?" Burns asked.

"Because he asked me to go have a beer with him. I don't know what makes him think I would want a beer, much less with a cretin like him."

Her taste probably ran more toward white wine and Perrier, Burns thought. And then he wondered if she might be hinting at something. He had lived a more or less celibate life in Pecan City for a long time, there not being an abundance of attractive unattached females around, and now he found himself attracted to two of them at the same time. His technique was rusty, but it was worth a try.

"Maybe you'd like to have a drink with me later on," he said. "There's a club at the Holiday Inn. We could have a little white wine, maybe dinner."

"That sounds nice. About seven-thirty."

"Uh, yes. Seven-thirty. Shall I meet you there or come by your room?"

"I'll meet you there," she said, giving him the old up-and-under. "I'm looking forward to it."

As Burns walked on to his car, he found himself hardly believing what was happening. He was investigating a murder, which was unusual enough in itself, but on top of that he seemed to have two dates in the same week, a record since his arrival in Pecan City. Things were definitely looking up.

He changed his mind the next morning, however. That was when he found the body of Harold Duncan. On the third floor of Main. In room 312, which just happened to be his own office. The dead pigeon was gone from the ledge, but Duncan was lying on the floor of the office, just as dead as the pigeon was.

"I just don't get it, Burns," Boss Napier said. He was sitting in a chair in Burns's office. The body of Harold Duncan had been carted away, finally, after a lot of investigation, and things in Main had calmed down somewhat. They would never quite be the same, however. Miller himself had mounted the three flights of stairs and done everything but tear his hair out. His first year as president of the school was obviously not working out exactly like he had planned.

Napier crossed his legs, showing off the ostrich quills on his boots. "How is it that a guy like you, who teaches stuff like *Silas Marina*—"

"*Marner*," Burns said.

"Yeah, that one. How can a guy like that get tangled up in so damn much trouble? That's what I'd like to know."

"Me too," Burns said.

"I tell you the truth, Burns, I'm disappointed. I thought you might could help me out on this one, you knowing the college people and all. It's hard for a cop to come on the campus and start asking questions, but you, I thought you could get away with it. But what happens? Another stiff."

Burns didn't like to think about the body. There was still a red stain on his rug where Duncan's head had rested. He had been shot, like Street, with a small-caliber gun.

"And of course you got you an alibi all ready, don't you?" Napier said.

"When did he die?" Burns asked.

"Now that's a good question. If you shot him, you'd know the answer, right? So that makes you innocent. Unless you're just a smart guy."

"I'm not a smart guy."

"I can believe it. Anyway, I don't know when he died. We'll have to let the doc tell us that. But I'd guess around midnight."

"Then I don't have an alibi." Burns's date with Melinda Land had ended about ten-thirty. They had drunk white wine, eaten a steak, and gone back to her room, where they had talked about teaching in a state university as opposed to a small private school, about the pitiable quality of the students they got these days, about why there had been no great American novels in the past twenty-five years.

They also drank a little more white wine, and Burns learned that all was not roses in the state universities. Though Melinda Land made a great deal more money than he did and had to teach only nine hours—three classes—per semester, she was under pressure to publish. She had not been as successful as her department head wished, and she was unlikely to get tenure unless she could get at least two articles accepted within the current academic year. In a way, Edward Street's murder was a godsend to her.

"Of course, I got to deliver my paper at your seminar, which was great and will probably count in my favor, but now I have a chance to do something really significant, especially if I can tie Street's death in to something directly from his books. If I can find how it fits the theme of death and dying, say. So I have to stay here until they find out who killed him. Then I'll have a unique approach to his works. It'll be a prestigious publication, I just know it."

Burns wished her well and drove home, but not before he received a sizzling kiss. He thought about it as he guided the big Plymouth through the quiet streets of Pecan City. By that time of night, everyone was at home and in bed. He did not pass more than two cars on his way back to his house, which was located at least five miles from the motel.

Burns had not been kissed like that in a long time. Too long. It woke his body up and made him realize what he had been missing. He was looking forward to seeing Melinda Land again.

"Hell," Napier said, trying to get comfortable in the chair, and bringing Burns out of his reverie. "It's better that you don't have an alibi, to tell the truth. If you had one, then I'd have to try to break it. This just makes it easier to me."

"Does that mean you think I killed Duncan?"

"Nope. I know you better than that, Burns. You wouldn't kill anybody. You just want to catch crooks and play like you're a tough guy, so you can forget what you really do for a living."

Yeah, and you play with kid's toys so you can forget what you do for your own living, Burns thought.

"So where does that leave us?" he said.

"Figuring out what Duncan was doing in your office," Napier said.

"I think he'd been in here before," Burns said. He told Napier about the way his desk had been rearranged.

"Did you ask the maid if she did it?"

"I haven't had a chance," Burns said.

"Well, ask her. Anything missing?"

Burns had looked around, though not carefully. Still, he did not believe anything was gone from his desk or shelves.

"No," he said. "Everything's here."

"What do you think he was after?"

Burns had no answer for that one at first. And then he thought about the books. "Do you think he might have been after those library books that were stolen?" he asked.

"Why? You got 'em?"

"No, but he might have thought I took them. Maybe he thought I was hiding them for some reason."

"Concealing evidence? Yeah, he might've thought that. That's like you, Burns."

Burns tried to look innocent, but he knew that he was guilty of exactly that in a sense. He still had not told Napier that Miller had been the last one to check the books out or that he might have seen them on Miller's shelves.

"Did Street have any visitors that night he died? Get any phone calls?" Burns asked.

"Funny you should mention that. We actually checked. I'm not stupid, you know."

"I know. I didn't mean to imply that you were."

"Sure you didn't. Anyway, nobody saw any visitors, and he didn't get any calls."

Burns looked disappointed.

"He did *make* a few calls, though," Napier said. "Called some friends of yours, as a matter of fact." He named off the people on Burns's list.

"Should I talk to them?" Burns said. "Ask them questions, I mean?" His mind was racing. Why hadn't either Clem or Mary mentioned anything about a phone call?

"I guess you can carry on, Burns, but there'll be some of my men involved in things now. There's been too much dying already. It's like you were some kinda jinx."

"Maybe nothing else will happen," Burns said.

"It better not," Napier said.

Burns decided to go down to the History lounge at noon on the off chance that Fox and Tomlin might be there.

He had missed his morning class, but he would teach the one that night, Burns supposed. No need to call it off just because there had been a murder in the building. He did not know whether other classes had been canceled or not.

One of the windows on the stair landing was open. The air conditioning in Main had never been particularly efficient, though it had been doing an adequate job lately. The smell was almost gone from Burns's office. Someone apparently didn't agree with Burns's opinion, however. People often opened the windows to try for a little cross-ventilation, despite the notes that Rose had taped to most of them. This one said:

PLEASE!
Do Not!!
OPen WinDows!!!
MaiD Rose

Burns pulled down the window and went on down to the History lounge. There was no one there when he entered. He looked at the sign on the wall, and he knew immediately that someone had been there at some time during the day. Someone had taken a black felt tip pen and blacked out the "L" so that the sign now read:

Burns figured it had to have been Tomlin who did it. Fox would never have dared.

"Admiring the artwork?" Tomlin said from behind him.

"Who did it?" Burns asked.

"The Phantom," Tomlin said. "Want a cigarette?"

"I want one," Burns said. "But I won't take one. Where's Fox?"

"In his office. Let's go."

"Why can't he come in here?"

"You'll see."

Burns followed Tomlin into the hall and down to Fox's office. They went in without knocking. Burns did not know exactly how the room had come into existence, but he thought the back of the classroom had been walled off to create it. It was more like a tunnel than an office. No more than eight feet wide, it was at least thirty feet long. Fox sat in the back, behind a makeshift room divider he had made from a portable bulletin board. There was a radio on his desk, and it was playing softly.

Fox wasn't wearing a shirt. It was obvious that he was never going to be a winner in the Arnold Schwarzenegger look-alike contest. He was hairy as a bear, and his body structure came more from fat than muscle.

"What's going on?" Burns asked.

"Earl had a little accident," Tomlin said. He got out a cigarette and lit it. "Let him tell you about it."

"I messed up my shirt," Fox said.

It was then that Burns noticed the shirt, though he couldn't say why or how he had missed it before. It was wet, and it was hanging across the top of the bulletin board. It was also typical of Fox's wardrobe. It had a white background, on which were displayed what looked like cattle, orange ones and tan ones, standing side by side. The orange cattle mostly concealed the tan ones.

"How can you tell you messed it up?" Burns asked.

Tomlin snorted.

"My pen leaked," Fox said. "I had to wash the shirt out in the lavatory."

Burns looked at Tomlin. "When did that happen?"

"This morning," Tomlin said. "But he taught his class. Don't worry."

"How?" Burns said, glad to hear that the murder hadn't disrupted the routine too much.

"He waited until after the bell had rung and they were all in there. Then he went in behind an opened umbrella."

Burns turned to Fox. "Is he kidding me?"

Fox didn't say anything.

"I'm not kidding," Tomlin said. "One of the students told me all about it. Said Dr. Fox peeked out at the room from behind the umbrella now and then during the lecture. Hard to believe, right?"

Burns laughed aloud. It sounded exactly like something Fox would do.

"Kind of embarrassing," Tomlin said, "but I guess it beats finding a dead man in your office."

Then, of course, Burns had to tell them all about it.

"So we've got two dead bodies now," Tomlin said when Burns was finished. "And it's all your fault."

"That's what Miller seems to think," Burns said. "At least he hasn't fired me."

"Yet," Fox said. He had put the wet shirt back on. It didn't look much worse than anything he usually wore.

"What's Boss Napier going to do about all this?" Tomlin said.

"He didn't say. He did tell me to ask Rose something, though." Burns got up. "I'll see you guys later."

"Sure you aren't sneaking over to the library for anything?" Tomlin said. "Get your card stamped, anything like that?"

"Not today," Burns said. He knew he was going to have

to take a bit of teasing about Elaine. That's why he had not said anything about Melinda Land.

He turned to leave and something on the radio caught his attention. "Turn that up," he said.

Fox reached for a dial and twisted it. The announcer's voice filled the office.

"This has truly been an unusual news day in our town," it said. "The murder at Hartley Gorman College is not the only event of note, as pigeons have been falling out of the sky all around the downtown area. One landed on the hood of a car parked outside a local jewelry store just as the owner was about to get out. The owner, Mrs. Merle Taupin, was so startled that she bumped her face on the steering wheel. Mrs. Taupin was treated for shock and a cut lip at Regional Hospital and released. In a related development, a dead cat was found beside the half-eaten carcass of a pigeon in an alley behind the Terrell Brothers Hardware Store. Authorities believe the pigeons to be toxic and warn that anyone sighting a dead pigeon should approach it with extreme caution. Anyone having information as to who might be poisoning pigeons within the city limits of Pecan City is asked to get in touch with local law enforcement officers. In other news—"

"You can turn it down," Burns said, and Fox twisted the dial again.

"You know anything about that?" Tomlin asked.

Burns was sure that Fairly was the guilty party. He had shot a few of the pigeons, but Fairly likely realized that he could never get them all that way. So he had put out poison. God knows how the attic would smell in a few days.

"Burns? What about it? You didn't poison those damn pigeons, did you?"

"No," Burns said. "Not me."

"But you know who did?"

"I'm afraid so," Burns said.

"Does it have anything to do with the murders?"

"Probably not," Burns said, hoping that he wasn't lying.

* * *

He found Rose on the first floor, where she was sweeping the front porch. She knew nothing at all about the moving of the materials on Burns's desk.

"No, sir. I didn't touch nothin' up there yesterday. I emptied your trash can in the mornin', but that was it. I didn't touch another thing."

Burns believed her. "Thanks, Rose. I was just wondering."

"Well, you don't have to wonder no more. And one othah thing. I don' think I'll be comin' up there for a while. I don' like bein' where no dead man's been."

"I could take care of the trash, I guess," Burns said.

"You can run the vacuum, too, if it gets done. I ain't goin' to be up there."

Burns didn't argue with her.

Miss Darling had been so shaken by the murder that she had asked for permission to go home early, but Clem was in her office, reading something in her freshman text and marking the page with a pencil. Burns waited until she had finished writing a marginal note before he asked why she hadn't mentioned her phone call from Street.

"Because I didn't get one," she said. "Is he supposed to have called me?"

"The police think so," Burns said. "They've probably checked the motel switchboard records for the numbers he called after the dinner Friday night."

"That's why I didn't get a call," Clem said, putting the book aside but holding on to the pencil. "I wasn't at home Friday night after the dinner."

Burns was surprised. Clem was his idea of the perfect old maid. She had never married and probably had never even considered it. She was a person who liked for everything to be done according to a schedule and for everything that had a place to be in that place. She did not tolerate any deviations from her routine, and she had the best course syllabuses Burns had ever seen. She never deviated from those, either, and she got truly furious when the former president of the school would dismiss all classes after ten o'clock on Friday if there was a big game coming up. The students and all the other teachers would be elated, but Clem would complain. Burns had never thought of her having a life outside of the school and her home. So where could she have gone after the dinner?

Clem noticed his look. "I was visiting a friend," she said.

Burns said, "I see."

"No, you do not see. I can tell that, Carl Burns. My friend is a member of the church. She had surgery, but she's home now. Her husband can't afford nursing care, so some of us have been taking turns sitting up with her until she's fully recovered. Friday night was my turn. If Edward Street called me, he didn't reach me."

"You didn't have to tell me that," Burns said. "I believed you." He didn't want to ask the next question, but he did anyway. "Why didn't you tell me the story about Street and Dick Hayes's current wife?"

Clem sniffed. Very few people could sniff effectively, but Clem was one of them. "That would be repeating gossip. You know that I don't like to repeat gossip. You're getting as bad as those policemen."

"Have they talked to you already?"

"Yes. And I didn't mention Dick Hayes to them, either."

That was all right with Burns. "Have you remembered any connection between Street and Mr. Fairly that you didn't tell me about earlier?" he asked. Then he added quickly, "That isn't gossip, I mean."

"Anything I said on that subject would be hearsay," Clem said.

"Is that as bad as gossip?"

Clem almost smiled. "It's close."

"Can you tell me anyway?"

Clem thought for a minute, toying with the pencil. Then she told him about the swimming pool.

·13·

Burns had heard any number of stories about the HGC swimming pool, but never the one that Clem told him now.

The indisputable facts were that there had once been an outdoor pool enjoyed in the proper season by faculty and students alike and that there was no longer such a pool.

No, the last fact was not indisputable. Actually, the pool still existed; it was simply impossible to enjoy it because it had been filled with dirt and covered up.

Summers in Pecan City were hot; so were springs and falls, usually. A pool could be used for quite a few months of the year, often from May until the end of October, and Burns had heard the stories of the faculty get-togethers held around the sides of the pool just before the beginning of school each year. He had heard of the fun the students had there, relaxing after a hard day of studies. (That one was a little more difficult for him to believe, but maybe students had studied harder in the days when the pool had been operative.)

All of that had come to an end, however, with the filling and the covering of the pool.

Burns had asked about it when he first arrived at HGC, and that was when he had first heard the stories. All of them agreed on one in particular. President Rogers had the pool filled, and the official story was that it had developed a leak that would cost thousands of dollars to repair. The school could not afford to waste money on such frivolous enterprises when money was desperately needed for the serious business of instruction, so the pool was simply disposed of.

Hardly anyone bought that story, and many other explanations for the pool's disappearance had sprung up. One such explanation held that parents visiting the school had been scandalized by the fact that male and female students were associating in the near-nude and had demanded the closing of the pool before there was a repetition of the Sodom and Gomorrah incident that they had read about in their Bibles.

Another, somewhat similar, version of the story had it that an irate mother had come down on the president's office like Byron's Assyrian, though without any gleaming cohorts, and threatened to sue the school because her daughter had been impregnated by the water in the pool.

It seemed that her daughter was as pure as a prairie flower and as innocent as the look in the eyes of a new-born doe; in short, she was a girl who had never known a young man, in the Biblical sense. Or so she had told her mother, who had then become convinced that the girl must have been somehow invaded by the rampant sperm in the college pool. How these itinerant sperm came to be there, the mother had no clear idea; but with impressionable young men swimming about, their heads filled with lustful thoughts, and scantily clad young women lounging around, anything would seem to be possible.

Burns liked both stories and would have been willing to believe either one of them, but to tell the truth neither of them struck the right chord of authenticity. However, the one Clem told sounded like it might be the correct one.

"Mr. Fairly was new here, it was his first year. He was young, as I think I told you earlier, and had never been to college himself. He did good work for the maintenance crew, though, and he did some of the odd jobs around this building, too. That's how he got to know Street."

"Nothing wrong with that," Burns said.

"No, but there were rumors that there was more to it than just a casual friendship."

Burns was astonished. "You mean to say that Street and Fairly were . . . were. . . ." He had to stop. He couldn't put his suspicions into words, not to Clem, despite what had happened only last year.

"Don't look like that," Clem said, slapping the pencil down on the desk. "I didn't mean to imply anything sexual."

Burns closed his mouth, which he realized had been drooping open. "What then?"

Clem looked sour. "The rest of this is purely gossip," she said, her lips thin.

"Tell me anyway. You've gone this far."

"Very well. The rumor was that Street, who was thought of as the campus radical in those days, occasionally smoked marijuana and that he offered to share some with Fairly. Fairly accepted. They weren't smoking in the building, mind you, but somewhere on the campus. Anyway, the story is that Fairly got rather high and offered Street a ride in the school's dump truck. This was in the winter and the pool had been drained. They were tooling around in the truck and Fairly lost control. It tore through the fence around the pool and kept right on going. Landed nose down in the shallow end. That's what cracked the pool."

"So the pool really is cracked?" Burns asked.

"I couldn't say. All I know is the story. You've heard the others?"

"A couple of them at least," Burns said.

"Maybe one of them is right. But you were asking about Street, so I told you."

"I don't understand, though," Burns said. "Why would that be something for Fairly to worry about? It wasn't his fault any more that it was Street's. In fact, Street was the one with the marijuana."

"That's right. And here's where the story gets hard to believe. According to what I heard, Street took all the blame. Fairly wasn't even there when Dirty Harry arrived on the scene. There was no one but Street in the truck. He had sent Fairly away and told him not to worry. Street claimed to have taken the truck himself and accepted sole responsibility for the wreck."

"I'm surprised Street wasn't fired," Burns said.

"So were a lot of other people," Clem said. "Knowing what we know now, I wonder if he had something on President Rogers."

It was certainly possible, Burns thought. "So if Street was really writing a book about HGC, he might have included the whole story and told who really wrecked the truck."

"It would be just like him," Clem agreed. "He would be in the book, of course. I can just see it—a noble, selfless young teacher, full of ideals, saving a poor, downtrodden member of the lower orders by doing a far, far better thing."

"Street was a regular Sidney Carton, all right," Burns said. "I'd really like to see that manuscript."

"I expect a lot of people would," Clem said. "I wonder where it is?"

Suddenly, so did Burns. He went looking for a telephone that he could use privately. He couldn't use his own office. The police weren't sure they were through in there, yet. Miss Darling was gone, so he used his pass key to get into Miss Darling's office. He was sure that she wouldn't mind, but he would tell her anyway. He knew he could have gotten in easily enough with a credit card, having gotten into his own office that way more than once, but he wanted everything to be on the up and up. That was always the best way.

"No, we didn't find any bunch of typing paper in Street's room," Napier said in answer to Burns's telephone query. "I've called the police where he lived and they've searched his house there, too. They found a lot of stuff, but nothing like you're talkin' about."

Burns should have known. He'd underestimated Napier again. This time, Clem had told the police chief about the letter she had received from Street, and the Boss had already checked it out.

"Do you think Street had it with him?" Burns asked. "That whoever killed him took it from his room?"

"You think I'm one of them psychics that get big bucks for readin' minds?" Napier said. "Is that it?"

"Well, no, but I—"

"Yeah, I know. You was wonderin' about it. You don't wonder, Burns. Leave that to me." Napier paused. "You know what I think?"

"No," Burns said. "What do you think?"

"I think maybe that's what Duncan was looking for in your office. You were the last person to see Street, as far as anyone knows, and someone could've told Duncan about the book."

Burns had not thought of that. "You mean Duncan thinks—thought—that I killed Street?"

"Nope. But he might've thought Street gave you the book. You're an English teacher, after all."

"Well, he didn't give it to me," Burns said. "Besides, Duncan probably didn't know about the book."

"You don't know that. You don't know what that guy knew. He might've found out. He was a reporter, wasn't he?

"Yes," Burns admitted.

"So he could've known. But I'll tell you something else. I don't even think Street wrote another book. I think he just started that rumor to scare people."

Burns thought about it and realized that Napier could be right. It made sense, considering the kind of man Street was, and it showed that Napier was a shrewd judge of people, even though he did not seem to be. The police chief was full of surprises.

"You've got a point," Burns said.

"Hell, yes, I do," Napier said. "From everything I hear, that Street was a real bastard. I'm just surprised somebody didn't kill him sooner."

"Me too," Burns said. "I wish they'd done it somewhere else, too."

"You said it," Napier agreed.

After Burns hung up he sat and doodled on a piece of scratch paper, trying to make sense of things.

Mary Winsor had not told him about her call from Street. Why? Or did she even get a call? Clem had been gone, and it was possible that the Winsors had been out as well.

Fairly had a connection with Street, all right, but it was a tenuous one. After all these years, who would care if a young member of the maintenance crew had smoked marijuana with Street and wrecked a truck in the school's swimming pool? Fairly did have a gun, however, and there were all those dead pigeons falling around Pecan City to demonstrate his disregard for at least one form of life.

And what about President Miller? Were those books on his shelf the ones that were missing from the library? If so, why were they there? Burns thought there might be a way he could get a look at them later if he had to. There was something else about Miller that was bothering Burns, too, but he couldn't quite pin it down.

Dick Hayes was another matter. He was not one of Burns's favorite people, simply because he was so relentlessly cheerful. He made Rebecca of Sunnybrook Farm look like Lizzie Borden; he made Norman Vincent Peale look like John Calvin. But he had made a successful marriage with the much younger woman who had taken his wife's place. Burns wondered if the rumor about the death of Hayes's wife had any validity, and he wondered if Street had indeed been the one to start it.

Burns decided it was time to have a talk with Dick Hayes, though he dreaded it. Hayes's unswerving good humor caused in Burns a constant desire to throw up whenever he had to spend more than two minutes with the man.

The Business Building was across the street to the north of Main, so Burns went downstairs and outside. There was a dead pigeon lying on the sidewalk, and Burns kicked it aside. He was going to have to talk to Fairly, too.

Melinda Land was getting out of a rental car when Burns reached the street. She was wearing a green dress that matched her eyes and clung to her in all the right places. Burns felt a long-forgotten stirring.

"Hello, Carl," she said, looking at him steadily with those eyes. "I thought you might call me today."

"Uh, I've been a little busy."

"Yes, I'm sure you have. I heard about poor Harold on the radio."

Poor Harold? Burns wondered if his hearing was getting bad. "I thought you hated him," he said.

"Not really. And I certainly didn't want him to *die*. It must have been terrible for you, though, all the questioning and trouble with the police. Do they know who shot him?"

"Not yet," Burns said.

"I assume it's connected to Edward Street's death, don't you?"

"I guess so. I just can't think of any reason why someone would want to shoot Duncan."

Melinda shivered, though the day was hot. "It's all so awful."

"It should make an interesting article for you," Burns said.

"Well, there is that to consider. I was going to talk to Miss Nelson again. I'm sure she knows more than she told me yesterday."

"Good luck," Burns said.

"Will I see you tonight?"

"Uh, I have a class tonight."

"Maybe tomorrow, then." She went on past him and into Main.

Burns went on across the street to the business building, not dreading his talk with Hayes quite so much now, but his apprehension returned when a man came out of the building and got into an unmarked car.

It was just as they said in the mystery novels Burns read—you could always spot a cop. The man getting into the car could be nothing else. He wore a cheap suit that looked a bit too small through the shoulders and a tie that seemed to choke him. The car was a nondescript Ford that looked exactly like every other city vehicle in town. Maybe the visit would have disturbed the seemingly imperturbable Hayes.

It was getting on toward the middle of the afternoon now, and the Business Building was practically deserted. It was almost impossible to get students to register for afternoon classes, though Burns, like every other department head, was required to schedule them. What usually happened was that only five or six students would sign up for the classes, which meant that the classes could not be run. It would not be economically feasible.

So Burns would have to go into the classroom on the first day and announce that there would be no class. The students who came were angry at the cancellation because they had carefully worked on their schedules to include the afternoon class; they would have taken it some other time if they could have. Burns was angry because the students were angry. The administrators were happy, however, because they could show the Board that afternoon classes had been scheduled, even if not enough students would take them.

Because there were very few afternoon classes, most faculty members worked out their office hours so that they could leave the campus by two or three o'clock. Some of the administrators did not like that, and they were fond of saying that they could shoot a shotgun down the hallways of Main at four o'clock and not hit a soul. Burns's answer to that was that he could shoot a shotgun through the administrative offices at seven o'clock in the morning when he arrived on campus and not hit anyone then, either.

The door to Hayes's office was open, but no one was in there. Burns stuck his head in the door and looked around. There were signs on the walls, all of them expressing Hayes's philosophy of life. One of them said, IF LIFE HANDS YOU A

LEMON, MAKE LEMONADE! Another said, I AIN'T MUCH, BABY, BUT I'M ALL I'VE GOT! There was one with a giant smiley face:

SMILE!

GOD LOVES YOU!

And there was one that sounded to Burns as if it might have come from some television evangelist, but which quoted without attribution: "Something GOOD is going to happen to YOU!"

Burns had bought a sign a year or so back. It said, "A Dirty Mind Is A Terrible Thing To Waste." He had never had the nerve to put it on his office wall, but he decided that he would do it the next day.

He went back out into the hallway, looking around. He didn't see anyone, but he heard something. There was an intermittent whipping or pounding noise coming from somewhere near the rear of the building.

Burns walked in the direction of the pounding. It was coming from the men's rest room.

Burns cautiously pushed the door open.

There was no one in the open area, but there was a pair of brown wing tip shoes showing underneath the door of the stall. The shoes were facing the toilet.

As Burns stood there he heard a long, loud grunt: "Unnnhhhhh!"

The sound was punctuated by a loud *whap*ping noise as something thrashed the toilet seat, which apparently bounced up and clicked back down.

Then the sounds were repeated:

"Unnnhhhhh!"

"WHAP!"

"Click."

There was silence for a few seconds, and Burns could hear a harsh panting. *Whoever was in there must have a hell of a digestive problem,* Burns thought.

The stall door opened and Dick Hayes stepped out, threading his belt through the loops on his dark blue pants. Hayes was short and completely bald, and he wore one of the worst toupees Burns had ever seen. It was some indeterminate shade between orange and brown and looked as if it might be made out of carpet remnants. Burns had once seen Hayes walking across the campus, and the toupee had been snagged by a very low-hanging limb. Hayes had not realized his hair was missing for several steps, and Burns thought a bird might nest in it if Hayes did not retrieve it.

Hayes looked up and saw Burns watching him. He was very much taken aback. "Oh, uh, I didn't know there was, uh, anyone in here, Burns. What happened to your nose?"

"Just happened to be passing by," Burns said, ignoring the remark about his nose. He was getting tired of hearing about his nose. "I thought someone might need help."

Hayes buckled his belt and smiled broadly. "Nosirree, no help needed. That was just my way of lettin' off a little steam. Y'see, Burns, I don't let life get me down. And if it starts to, well, I just do something about it. Like now. I was gettin' a little bit tense and needed to unwind, so that's what I came in here to do. Now I feel great! You can't let things get you down."

First it was Elaine and bubble-blowing, now it was Hayes with the belt. The signs had been bad enough.

"Yessir, I just come in here to the old restroom and take off my belt and whale the tar out of that old commode in there," Hayes went on. "Doesn't hurt the commode, y'see, and it's a lot better than hittin' a person, don't you think?"

"Sure," Burns said. "Especially if the person's a cop."

Hayes's smile collapsed. His fingers twitched in the direction of his belt buckle. "Who told you there was a cop in here?"

"I saw him," Burns said.

"Oh," Hayes said. "Well, naturally they wanted to talk to me about old Ed Street. Speed, we used to call him. He liked that. I couldn't help them any, though." He looked around the restroom. "Why don't we get out of here, Burns? If you came by to visit, we can do that in my office."

Burns started to say that he found the atmosphere more congenial in the rest room, but he thought better of it. They left the rest room and returned to Hayes's office.

Hayes settled himself into the executive chair behind his desk, and Burns sat in the visitor's chair.

"Now what's this about you dropping by?" Hayes said, his hand smoothing his toupee. His smile was back in place. "You don't make a habit of visiting the business department very often."

"I was wondering if you told the cop about your call from Street," Burns said.

The smile disappeared again. "He already knew about it. How did you find out?"

"I heard," Burns said vaguely. "Did he happen to ask you anything about the rumor concerning your late wife?"

"Now just a minute, Burns," Hayes said, standing up to his full height, which wasn't much over five-six. "What gives you the right to come in here and say things like that?"

"President Miller asked me to look into things. He said I could be assured of the full cooperation of the faculty. Do you want to call him and check it out?" Burns knew Hayes wouldn't call. Everyone at HGC was deathly afraid of losing his job; no one would question the president.

Hayes forced the smile back into place. "No, no. Of

course not. If President Miller wants cooperation, he can always count on me. You can tell him that, Burns."

"I will," Burns lied. "Now about that rumor. . . ."

"That was a vicious lie," Hayes said. He was sweating now, and Burns saw a trickle of moisture running out from under the toupee. "I didn't mention it because it was nothing more than slander. I never knew that Street started the rumor, either, if that's what you're implying."

"But you thought he did," Burns said. "Exactly how did your first wife die, anyway?"

"Cancer," Hayes said. "It was terrible, Burns, terrible. If it hadn't been for Traci, I would never have been able to survive the ordeal." Traci was the student Hayes had married. "I know it sounds phony, but I deeply loved my wife, and I deeply love Traci. We never even so much as held hands until months after my wife died."

"And Street had his eye on Traci, too."

"Yes. She was in one of his classes. But he had his eye on all the girls. I shudder to think of the co-eds he might have ruined if he'd been teaching at a state university."

It was an article of faith among HGC teachers that state universities were hotbeds of sin and corruption, and no matter what happened at HGC to demonstrate that the same things that happened at larger state schools also happened at the smaller private ones, still, no one at HGC would admit it.

"Did you happen to talk to that reporter who was killed?"

"I did. I told the police all about it. They wanted to know about a letter and a phone call I got, too. I told them that."

"What was the call about?"

"It was just Street telling me about the book he was working on. Things like that." Hayes suddenly reached up and pulled off his toupee with his left hand. He pulled a tissue from a box on his desk and ran it across the top of his sweating head.

"Did he mention anything that was going to be in the book?"

"A couple of things." Hayes settled the toupee back into place.

"What things?"

The smile faded. Burns had never seen Hayes look so gloomy. "Things he shouldn't be putting in there, things about his affair with Mary Winsor, about Abner Swan's affair with the choir director of his church—"

"Wait a minute, wait a minute," Burns said, holding up a hand. He couldn't believe what he was hearing. "You're saying that Abner Swan and Mary Winsor each had affairs?"

"I'm not saying it. Street said it."

Mary certainly hadn't mentioned anything about an affair with Street. "What about you and your first wife?"

"That was going to be in there, too."

Good grief, Burns thought. "Is there anyone he missed?"

"Not that I know of." Hayes tried valiantly to get his smile back. "None of it was true, as far as I know. He was just being himself."

"And you talked to the reporter who got killed last night?"

"Just for a little while." Hayes's attempted smile was gone. "He tricked me."

"How?" Burns said.

"Told me about the letter he got. Made me think it was the same as mine."

"You mean he knew about the book Street was writing?"

"I guess he did. I told him."

Well, Burns thought, *score another point for Boss Napier.*

·14·

Burns could not get any more information out of Hayes, who spent nearly twenty minutes explaining that his first wife had been under constant medical observation for the last four months of her life, and had in fact been confined to the local hospital. There was no way Hayes could have had anything to do with her death.

"So what does Street say about it in the book?"

"Well, you know how people have a way of twisting things."

"No," Burns said, feeling hard and ruthless, like he imagined Philip Marlowe must have felt on occasion. "Why don't you tell me?"

"He hinted that he was going to say that I—the character in the novel, I mean, not really me—that I slipped into the hospital and injected an air bubble into her vein."

"But that never occurred to you," Burns said.

"Of course not. I love life." Hayes looked around at his signs. "I would never deprive anyone of his or her chance at it, even someone in pain. Street was a crazy man. I don't know how he ever came up with anything like that."

Burns had a pretty good idea. He knew a little something about the way writers worked, which was just the same way anyone worked if he had a story to tell. They left out the boring things, intensified the interesting things, and made up a lot of things out of thin air.

Burns left Hayes in the office looking at his signs for comfort. For some reason, Burns was feeling even more depressed than he had been when he entered. *Smile,* he told himself. *Something good is going to happen to YOU!*

Nothing good did, however. He went by the library, where Elaine was supervising the clean-up of the stacks. She didn't have time to talk to him, and he wasn't even bothered. He found himself thinking of Melinda Land and wishing that he didn't have an evening class.

He went to talk to Mary Winsor and point out that she had not been completely frank with him, but she was not in her office. A student-secretary told Burns that she had been called home because of an emergency. Her cat had somehow gotten trapped in the neighbor's dryer vent. Burns might not have believed that had it been anyone except Mary.

He was about to leave when the phone rang. The student answered it and said, "He's right here." He handed the telephone to Burns. "It's your office," he said.

Burns could not imagine who would be calling from his office, but it was Bunni. "I thought I saw you walking across the street," she said. She spent a lot of time looking out the window of the third floor when she was supposed to be performing her secretarial duties. The truth was that there were not that many duties to perform. "Dr. Elliott is looking for you. I told him to wait in your office."

"I'll be right there," Burns said. He needed to talk to Elliott anyway. His name was on the list.

* * *

"Ah," Elliott said when Burns got to the third floor. "I've been hoping to talk to you. I couldn't get in your office, however."

"We can use Miss Darling's office," Burns said. He opened the door with the pass key and they went in. Burns sat behind Miss Darling's desk. "What's the problem?"

"No problem," Elliott said. "May I close the door?"

"Of course," Burns said. Elliott always wanted to close the door when he had something confidential to say, no matter how trivial.

After he had shut the door, Elliott sat back down. "Two things, Burns." He always enumerated the number of his points. "First, I want you to know I enjoyed the seminar very much."

Elliott was something of a brown-noser, though not nearly in the same class as Abner Swan.

"Thank you," Burns said. "I'm afraid our guest of honor didn't."

"No, and I'm quite sorry about that, Burns. In fact, that's what I really wanted to discuss with you."

Burns had suspected as much. Elliott was not merely a brown-noser; he was adept at covering his own ass when trouble loomed.

"Go on," Burns said.

"I suppose you may have heard about the book Street was purported to have been writing."

"I've heard."

"Then you may also have heard that it involves some of the people who are currently teaching here at HGC."

"I've heard that, too."

"Have you by any chance heard what's in it?"

"Some things."

"What things?" There was a definite quaver in Elliott's usually self-assured tones.

"I'd rather not say," Burns told him. "Some of them weren't exactly flattering to people who teach here."

"Yes," Elliott said. "I know. It may surprise you, Burns, to know that I am one of those people."

"Not really," Burns said.

Elliott looked at him suspiciously. "I know that you're working for President Miller on this," he said. "What did he tell you about me?"

"Nothing," Burns said. He was always amazed at how fast the news got around at HGC. It was almost as if the offices were bugged, or that some of the faculty members were psychic.

"Come on, Burns," Elliott said. "He must have said something."

"Nothing. Why don't you enlighten me?"

Elliott looked around as if to make sure the door was tightly shut. Satisfied, he turned back to Burns. "Street called me the other night, after the dinner. He hinted that he had used a character based on me in an unfinished book and that the character was going to be somewhat unflattering. He was going to make him—the character, I mean—a toady of the administration, someone who informed on others for his own benefit."

"No!" Burns said. He was convinced that Elliott was not above such practices and that the man had gotten his current position, supervisor of one of the men's dorms—a position which included both room and board in addition to his teaching salary—as a payoff for delivering the goods in the hiring of a certain dean. If a man would do that, he would certainly inform.

Elliott nodded. "I know it's inconceivable, but that's what he said. He said the book would show me in the worst possible light."

"And you're worried about that?"

"No. Of course not. Everyone would know at once that it was a total fabrication. I'm worried about what he might have said about everyone else."

"I see," Burns said, though he wasn't sure he did. If Elliott was telling the truth, he was getting off much lighter than anyone else Burns had heard about. "So you're concerned only with the effect of the book on others."

"That is correct. Naturally it could have no effect on me. And I was thinking that if you happened to run across the manuscript, it might be best if you simply destroyed it. You could save many good people a great deal of anguish."

Not the least of whom would be you, Burns thought. It was obvious that despite his protestations to the contrary, Elliott did not want the book to be seen. If it were, then everyone would have his suspicions confirmed about him, not that there was any doubt. Seeing it in print was more convincing than merely believing in your heart, however.

Elliott talked for a few minutes longer, then left. It was clear to Burns that people were beginning to get the wind up over the missing manuscript, and Elliott seemed to think that Burns might have found it, or might find it later. And if Elliott felt that way, Duncan may well have reached the same conclusion.

It was too late in the afternoon to go home, so Burns decided to stay at school until after his evening class. He walked around to see if Bunni was still at her post. She was not there. There was a note on the desk saying that she did not feel like staying in the building alone and that she would not enter the hours on her pay form.

Burns did not blame her for leaving. The old building got lonesome sometimes, and to sit there close to the room where a man had been killed the previous night was not easy to do. Burns wasn't especially looking forward to going back into his own office when the police finally decided to let him.

He returned to the other hall and got a book out of one of the shelves that served as departmental mailboxes. Napier had let him remove the books he would need for teaching from the office, and that night he was going to discuss *The Great Gatsby.* He always liked to start his course in American novels with Hemingway and Fitzgerald and lull the students into a false sense of security, letting them think that all the books would be as easy to read as the first ones. Then he would hit them with Faulkner. *The Sound and the Fury* usually came as something of a shocker.

He took the Fitzgerald book into Miss Darling's office and thumbed through it. He could hear the usual noises of the old building, but there was no longer the pitter-patter of tiny talons above his head. He wondered how many little pigeon carcasses there were up there, smoldering away like John Brown's body.

Then he began thinking about a list he wanted to make, the ten worst movies made from the ten best books. He thought that the Robert Redford version of *The Great Gatsby* would make a good starting place. Sure, the yellow car was nice, and so were Redford's smile and his gorgeous rag of a pink suit, but that was about it. He really did not make a very good Gatsby, much less a great one. And Mia Farrow as Daisy? Who were they kidding?

Too bad they didn't consult me about these things, Burns thought, taking another piece of Miss Darling's scratch paper. Before long he had added "*The Sun Also Rises* (the one with Tyrone Power)" to the list, along with "any Matt Helm movie with Dean Martin" and "Bill Murray's *The Razor's Edge*." Once you got started on something like that, you could think of plenty of titles. Before he knew it, it was time for class.

Evening classes at HGC were supposed to run from six-thirty until nine-thirty. Everyone knew, however, that to keep the classes for three hours was unfair to everyone. Regular classes met for only fifty minutes a day Monday, Wednesday, and Friday, which equaled two and a half hours per week. So no one ever kept evening classes longer than nine o'clock, unless there was an unusually long break in the middle. Burns gave hardly any break at all, just enough time for everyone who wanted to get a drink to jog down the three flights, then jog back up. He usually put his book back on the shelf at nine o'clock on the dot.

A plan had been taking shape in his mind most of the afternoon, a plan for getting a look at the books in Miller's office. He was convinced that the copies of Street's books had come from the library. They had to be the same ones. After all, Miller was the only one who hadn't asked Burns about his nose when he first saw him after the fight in the library. Burns was convinced that Miller hadn't said anything because he had known already that Burns had a broken nose. He had known because he was the one who had broken it.

There was no way to get into Miller's office when school was in session. The secretary would not let him in there if Miller was out, and he certainly didn't want to do anything if Miller was there. It was obvious that he had to get into the office when no one was there at all. Say, in the evening.

There were two obstacles to that plan. One was Dirty Harry, the campus security. That obstacle could be easily disregarded. Harry had a chair in the boiler room, and there he sat, winter and summer, all night long. If you blundered into him, you took the risk of getting shot, but there was not much chance that he was going to be checking the buildings as he was supposed to be doing.

The other obstacle was the warehouse where the offices were located. Burns had to get inside it. Once inside it, he had to get into Miller's office, but he would worry about that if he got into the warehouse. He thought about calling Napier and getting police help, but that would complicate things no end. There were legalities like search warrants and things for which Napier would no doubt be a stickler, whereas those things didn't bother Burns at all. And besides, Burns hadn't mentioned to Napier his suspicion that the books might be in Miller's office. No need to go into all that now.

Burns waited until his students had left Main, then started down the stairs. He thought he heard someone, so he stopped and waited. No one came along. He called out, but there was no answer. He wondered if the building had bats in the attic now. He waited for several minutes, but when no one came, he went on down and out the front door.

His car was parked in the street, but he decided to walk. It would be easier to lose himself in the shadows. The car was too easily identified as his. How many 1967 Plymouth Furies were still roaming the streets, anyway?

One of Pecan City's main streets ran in front of the warehouse, and there was a bright streetlight on the corner. But behind the building there was only a gravel road that trucks had used to get to the loading dock when the warehouse was still a warehouse, and there were no lights at all. That darkened area was where Burns was headed.

He looked around when he reached the streetlight, but he didn't see anyone except for a dark figure near the library. That was probably just a student who had studied late and was leaving for home, no one for him to worry about.

The side of the warehouse was in darkness. It faced the railroad tracks that Burns had often cursed when he was in a hurry only to find himself waiting for a train that seemed ten miles long. Now the tracks were helping him, since there were no houses nearby. He walked over the rough rocks beside the tracks, not going fast because he didn't want to fall. Soon he was behind the warehouse.

He saw the black outline of the loading dock and approached it cautiously. There was a sliding metal door there, but it was closed and presumably locked. That wasn't where he hoped to enter. It seemed to him, however, that he had seen a couple of windows the other day when he went to Miller's office and was looking around the warehouse. One of them had a broken pane that was covered with nothing sturdier than cardboard. If he could remove the cardboard and unlatch the window, he could raise it and go inside.

There was a problem, though. The loading dock, not much wider than the back of a delivery truck, did not run beneath the windows, which was probably why no one had really bothered to replace the glass. Had Burns been standing on the dock, he could have reached the windows; as it was, although he could reach the window and even move the cardboard aside, he couldn't reach the latch.

He looked around for something to stand on.

There wasn't anything.

He looked across the gravel road. There was an unkempt field there, badly in need of mowing. Beyond the field the railroad track circled back on the town, and beyond the track were houses. No one in the houses would be looking in Burns's direction, and if they were, they couldn't see him. He crossed the road and started walking down the shallow ditch that ran beside it, hoping that someone had thrown away something useful there.

He hadn't walked far before he found a bucket that had once held roofing tar, probably tossed there a year or so before when the warehouse roof had been repaired. Silently thanking the workman who had not been conscientious about cleaning up, he carried the bucket back to the windows.

Standing on the bucket and straining mightily, he got his arm inside all the way up to the shoulder. His fingers barely reached the latch. For a second he thought he might not be able to free it, but he did. Then he pushed the window up. It was as easy as that.

Getting inside was a little trickier, but he hoisted himself up over the window ledge and then he was inside the warehouse.

It was pitch dark. The only light came from the window, and that was almost no light at all. Burns thought he had read somewhere that you should leave a light on in buildings at night to discourage burglars. Maybe he would bring that up at the next faculty meeting.

Then again, maybe he wouldn't.

He started moving across the warehouse, trying not to bump into things. What things, he couldn't really say. There were riding lawn mowers, leaf blowers, wooden pallets stacked high with paper to be used in copiers and by the instructional services area, tools of all kinds. He had seen that much on his former visits to the place in daylight. In the dark, however, everything looked pretty much alike, nothing more than bulky outlines of darkness.

He finally got to Miller's office, having stubbed his toe

only once and disgusted because he hadn't brought a flashlight. Once in Miller's office, with the door safely closed, he would turn on the lights.

Getting in the office was not hard. The old credit card worked fine, just the way it did for the private eyes in books. One reason it did was that the doorknobs on many of the doors at HGC had been put on wrong. Someone had once explained to Burns that if the smooth side of the key faced up when you inserted it into the lock, there had been a mistake made. Burns didn't know what difference it made, except that the doors were easier to open with a credit card.

In Miller's outer office, he closed the door behind him and turned on the light. He stood there for a few seconds, blinking, and then he went on into the inner sanctum, which thoughtfully had been left open for him.

He turned on the light in there and looked at the bookshelves. Street's books were right there where he had seen them, and he walked over and pulled them off the shelves. He opened *Dying Voices* and saw the red-stained pages. He looked at them more closely than he had in the library and ran his fingers over the stains. Now that he had time to inspect them, he would have sworn that they were not blood at all—not that he had ever thought they were—but some kind of paint.

So why had Miller taken the books? Had he painted the pages as some sort of protest against Street, then lost the courage of his convictions? Or had he killed Street and then been afraid that the books would lead directly to him, having forgotten until too late that the library would have a record of who checked the books out?

It didn't matter. Finding that out was Napier's job. Burns would deliver the books to the police chief and let him have all the glory of solving the case.

Or maybe not. he didn't want to do anything too hastily. First, he would confront Miller and see if the president had an explanation. *Then* he would go to Napier.

He turned off the light and went into the outer office. He looked around, but he had left nothing behind to show he had been there. After he had turned that light off as well, he stood for a while, trying to let his eyes adjust to the darkness. He could have been deep in a cave for all the light there was. He would be able to see at least the outlines of the things in the warehouse and avoid falling over them.

He had just started to open the door when he heard a noise in the warehouse.

· 15 ·

Burns's hand froze to the doorknob. He had heard a dull thud, followed by the sound of metal scraping on the concrete floor of the warehouse. Or that was what he thought he had heard. It was hard to be sure. The sound had been muffled by the door, and he was already nervous about being alone in the building. Maybe he hadn't heard anything at all.

He stood as still as he could, listening. He realized that he was sweating. He felt a drop run out of one of his sideburns and onto his cheek. *Just the heat in the building,* he told himself. No air conditioning at night, so naturally it was hot in there. That was all. It wasn't that he was scared.

He waited for what seemed like forever, and then he found himself counting off the seconds. He discovered that a minute could be a very long time under certain circumstances.

He wondered what he should do. He couldn't stay in the office forever. It would be pretty hard to explain to the secretary what he was doing there when she came in the next morning.

"Oh, good morning, Miss Reeves. I just thought I'd drop

by to say hello. Heh-heh. What? The books. Oh, I was just going to return them to the library for Dr. Miller. I'll be going now."

He knew it would never work. He was going to have to get out of there.

He turned the knob slowly, slowly. When it had gone as far as it could go, he began to open the door, even more slowly than he had turned the knob.

He opened it only far enough so that he could squeeze through the crack, and he didn't bother to close it behind him. He had gotten only a step away, however, when it began to swing shut, sounding to Burns as if a banshee had been unleashed in the building. He reached back and grabbed the edge of the door, nearly dropping the books.

He shut the door as slowly as he could, and there was no more screeching. Clutching the books to his chest, he started across the warehouse in the direction of the window, which he could see as a dim square of lighter darkness. The only comfort he had was the fact that if there was someone in there with him, of which he wasn't really sure, then whoever it was—unless one of his close relatives was a cat—couldn't see any better than Burns could.

He was moving along with some success, not having kicked a stack of paper or fallen over a lawn mower. He thought he could make it to the window easily.

Then his foot hit something. He was never sure what it was, though it was something low and close to the floor, something like the end of one of the pallets that the paper rested on. It didn't hurt, but he did emit a small grunt.

That was when the light hit him in the face. It was coming from a level about three feet higher than his head, as if someone were lying on top of one of the stacks of paper. It was quite a bright light, and Burns was momentarily blinded.

It was just as well that he was. That way, he didn't know that he was going to be shot until he heard the gun. There was a flash of flame and then something slammed into Burns's chest, knocking him backward into a riding lawn mower. It was a huge Snapper, almost as big as a Daihatsu. Burns crashed into it, dropping the books he had been holding and cracking his head on the driver's seat.

As he lay there, barely conscious, he could hear something scrambling across the top of the boxes.

It's Fairly, he thought. *Coming to finish me off.*

There was a sharp pain in his chest, and he tried to reach it with his hand, but he found it too difficult to move even that much.

Someone was shining the light on the floor nearby, but Burns couldn't see who it was. His eyes were barely open.

He thought he was probably dying, but he really didn't care.

There was a scraping sound as someone moved a book, and Burns heard an exclamation of disgust, though not enough of one to identify the voice.

There was a thud as the book was tossed back to the floor, and that was the last Burns knew for a while. His head lolled to the side, his eyes closed, and he lost consciousness completely.

When Burns woke up again, he thought at first that he was having a heart attack. His head hurt, but his chest hurt even more. *It was death,* he thought, *sitting on my chest. Death had a snout like a hyena, and he could smell the stinking bastard's breath—*

He shook himself out of "The Snows of Kilimanjaro" and opened his eyes. It was still pitch dark in the warehouse, and he was alive. Whoever had shot him was gone.

His hand went out and touched one of the books. He felt around and found the other one. He had been shot for nothing.

Or maybe he hadn't been shot. He didn't seem to be bleeding or anything. He tried to touch his chest, and this time he was successful. There was no blood.

He took one of the books. Sure enough, there was a hole in it. There was a hole in the other one, too. Burns was silently thankful that *We All Die Today!* was nearly six hundred pages long and printed on thick, quality paper with good board wrappers. *Dying Voices* alone would never have saved him.

He tried to sit up and found he could do so without his head falling off. He took the books and stood. He was a little wobbly, but otherwise in pretty good shape.

He started for the window. It seemed like a long way, but he finally made it.

Climbing out was a bit harder. He dropped the books outside, then stepped through, turning and holding onto the window ledge.

The bucket was still there. He balanced on it and closed the window, but he did not try to lock it. He doubted that anyone would ever notice that it had been opened. He wasn't sure whether he had locked the door to Miller's office, but that didn't matter. The secretary would think she had left it unlocked. The only one who would know that something was wrong was Miller, when he saw that the books were gone.

Burns looked at his watch, but it was too dark for him to make out the hands. He would have to wait until he got to the streetlight.

He stood for a minute, trying to decide what to do. He was sure someone had tried to kill him, but who? And why?

His first thought had been Fairly, because he knew Fairly had a gun and because he associated Fairly with the ware-house, but maybe it hadn't been Fairly. Maybe it had been Miller. But wouldn't Miller have taken the books? Whoever had shot him definitely had not wanted the books.

And what was he going to do with the books? The bullet that had shot him—nearly shot him, he corrected himself—might be lodged in one of them. The books were evidence of attempted murder. Should he take them to Napier and tell him what happened as he had first thought, before he was shot at, or should he confront Miller?

All the thinking was making his head hurt worse. He plodded around the building and into the light. Glancing again at his watch, he saw that it was only ten o'clock. Miller would still be awake, and his house was not far away. Burns decided to go there first.

The President's Mansion wasn't really much of a mansion, but it was one of the oldest homes in Pecan City, having been built early in the century by a wealthy citizen who wanted to show off his good taste. It was more or less in the style of an antebellum Southern home, three stories tall, with columns and large pecan trees in the front yard. It was only a block from Main, so the president could walk to campus every day. Not that Miller ever did.

Burns walked to the house, however, figuring that the extra block would help to clear his head, which had developed a peculiar buzzing noise as he walked.

There were still lights on in the house, and Burns made his way up the walk, pushing aside a tricycle and a red Radio Flyer as he went. Miller was older than Burns, mid-forties probably, but he had two young children. Burns couldn't recall their ages, but he thought they were about three and five. Burns had long ago decided that if he ever got married, he would not have children. He was sure he had gotten too old to tolerate tricycles on the sidewalk. He wondered briefly what Elaine or Melinda thought about children, but by then he was on the porch and ringing the doorbell.

Mrs. Miller came to the door. She looked stressed. Her hair was a mess, and she was wearing a purple chenille robe belted around the middle.

"Yes?" she said, clearly not recognizing Burns. He had met her only once, at the annual fall picnic.

He told her who he was and said that he wanted to talk to her husband.

"We're trying to get the boys to bed," she told him. "Come in."

Burns went inside. The hardwood floors gleamed, and the stairway to the upper floors was polished to a high shine. One of the benefits of being president was that you got maid service, and free help from the maintenance crew whenever anything went wrong.

"I'll go up and tell him you're here," Mrs. Miller said, starting up the stairs.

After a few minutes there was a loud yell from above. "But I want *Daddy* to tell the story!"

Burns, and some of the other faculty members had wondered why Miller had not hosted an open house to introduce his family to the faculty. Now Burns was beginning to understand. He had somehow thought that college presidents led lives that were different from those of ordinary men. He should have known better.

Miller came down the stairs. He was wearing navy blue pajamas and a navy robe. He looked tired, but he perked up when he saw the books in Burns's hands.

"Where did you get those?" he demanded.

"Is there somewhere that we can talk?" Burns asked, not wanting to answer the question.

"This way," Miller said, leading Burns through a doorway and into a room that looked like a study. There was a desk, and the walls were lined with bookshelves, most of them empty. There were throw rugs on the floor.

"I asked you where you got those books," Miller said, turning to confront Burns.

Burns went on the offensive. "A better question might be where did *you* get them?"

Miller turned his face away. "I . . . ah, I got them from, ah, . . ." He turned back. "Oh, what the hel—heck. I'm sorry about your nose, Burns."

"So am I. Why did you do it?"

"I was in a state of shock. When I found out Street had been killed, I realized that someone might find out what had happened to the books and misinterpret it. I had to get them back. I never intended to return them to the library, but I put them down in the outer office and Miss Reeves thought I meant for her to check them in. I was going to replace them, you see."

"Replace them?"

"Well of course," Miller said. "Can't you see they're damaged?"

"I can see that, all right," Burns said. "What I wanted to know is why you did it."

"I didn't do it," Miller said. There was the thin edge of a whine in his voice. "That's why I knew I had to get them back. I followed you and Miss Tanner to the library, and when I saw that you were looking at the books, I panicked. I didn't want to hit you. It was just something that happened."

"If you didn't do it, who did?" Burns asked.

Miller looked at the ceiling of the room. "They did."

"They?"

"The boys," Miller sighed. "Don't you know finger-paint when you see it? I checked the books out to read before the seminar, and I left them in here on the desk. The boys found them one day and decided to decorate them. They used finger-paint."

"Oh," Burns said. "Finger-paint."

"That's right. Nothing sinister. No one was trying to send a message to Street. It was just two playful boys. But you can see how it might be misinterpreted."

Burns could see, all right.

"You aren't going to make a big thing of this, are you, Burns?"

"No, I don't guess I will," Burns said.

"Good." Miller's voice toughened. "Then explain where you got the books."

"In your office."

"What? You entered my office without permission?"

"That's right," Burns said. "And someone tried to kill me."

It took a while for Burns to tell the story, but it was clear that Miller hadn't had anything to do with the shooting.

"I started trying to get those little bas—devils to bed two hours ago," he told Burns. "You can ask my wife."

Burns didn't think that would be necessary, but he still

couldn't figure out why someone had tried to kill him. He would have to discuss it with Napier.

"Look, Burns," Miller said, "I can see why you were suspicious when you saw the books in my office, but you should certainly have asked me about them instead of creeping around like a common thief. Now that you know what happened, I insist that you keep my name out of this if you talk to the police."

"I'll try," Burns said. "Some of it will have to come out. Boss Napier will want to know what I was doing in your office, just like you did."

Miller groaned. "Well, at least keep it out of the newspapers."

"I can promise that, I think," Burns said.

Burns didn't know much about Napier's hours, but he figured that on a Tuesday night the chief might get home fairly early. Sure enough, there were lights on in Napier's home just as there had been in Miller's.

Napier came to the door. "Damn, Burns. I would've thought you'd be in bed by now."

"I have to talk to you," Burns said.

"Come on in, then. I was doing a little painting."

They went to the table, which was laid out with figures, paint, and brushes like before.

"You bring any tacos?" Napier asked.

"Not this time. Just these books." Burns went on and told the whole story while Napier rolled a figure of a cowboy around in his fingers.

"For an English teacher, you sure do get in a lot of trouble," Napier said when Burns had finished. "Lemme see the books."

Burns gave them to him, and Napier looked them over. "The slug's still in there," he said. "That's good. We can compare it with the one we dug out of Street."

"A .22, right?"

"Not necessarily," Napier said. "We don't do our own

• 153 •

ballistics work, and that was just a guess. Could've been a .32. Something small, anyway. We should know in a day or two. I'll keep these books."

That was all right with Burns.

"You got anything else you want to tell me?" Napier said.

"I don't think so. Your men have been ahead of me everywhere I go."

"Yeah, but people don't like to talk to them much." Napier got up and went to his refrigerator. He opened it and took out a two-liter bottle of Diet Coke. "You want a drink?"

Burns hated diet drinks. "Sure," he said.

Napier poured Coke into two glasses that he must have gotten in some kind of deal at a fast food outlet. The glasses had pictures of Elmer Fudd and Daffy Duck on them.

"I've been thinking," Burns said, taking a sip and trying not to make a face at the taste.

"Glad to hear it," Napier said. "What about?"

"About what I'm trying to find out. I'd nearly forgotten one thing."

"What's that?"

"Who wrote that letter to Duncan. I've been assuming that whoever wrote the letter must have defaced the books, but Miller's little boys surely didn't write it. Anyway, what I'm trying to say is that whoever wrote the letter didn't necessarily kill Street."

Napier finished off his Diet Coke and put the glass in the sink. "You're doin' good, Burns. People who write letters usually just write letters. They don't go killin' anybody. Usually they're sneaky assholes who wouldn't dare do anything they might get caught at."

"You didn't say anything about that before," Burns said.

"You didn't ask me. If you're gonna play Junior G-Man, you'll have to find out things for yourself."

"Thanks," Burns said, taking another small swallow of the drink. "At least we've solved one mystery, though. We know who broke my nose. Anything else you haven't told me?"

"Yeah. Take care of yourself. You might get shot if you're not careful."

"Thanks," Burns said. "I appreciate your concern."

"Don't mention it," Napier said. "I sure do wish you'd brought some tacos, though."

·16·

When Burns got out of his early class the next morning he went immediately to the History lounge to talk to Fox
and Tomlin. He wasn't going to tell them about his little adventure the night before unless they asked about the murders,
and as it turned out there was no danger of that. They had
other things on their minds. Tomlin was smoking, and Fox
was staring glumly at the altered "No Smoking" sign on the
wall.

"We're going to get in big trouble about that sign," Fox
said. "You can mark my words."

"Not me," Tomlin said. "I didn't do it." His face wore a
mask of innocence. It was an easy mask for him to assume,
and Burns didn't trust him for an instant.

"Well, I certainly didn't do it," Fox said. He was never
quite sure how to take Tomlin.

"The Phantom did it," Burns said.

"That's probably who's killing the pigeons, too," Tomlin
said. "I found a couple on the way in this morning. We can
blame it on the Phantom."

Fox wasn't buying it. "You two can joke about it all you

want to, but that won't help us when we get called to the president's office to explain things."

"We just won't go, then," Tomlin said, breathing out a plume of smoke. "Come on, Earl. Don't be such a worry wart. Have a smoke." He offered Fox his pack.

Fox waved the pack away. "No thanks," he said. "I've got my own." He didn't take them out, however.

"He's worried because of the latest dictum," Tomlin said, looking at the smoke wreathing the light fixture.

Burns didn't know what they were talking about. "What dictum?" he said.

"You didn't look in your mailbox?" Fox said. "No wonder you never know what's going on."

"I still can't use my office," Burns said. "I sat in a classroom and read the paper this morning until eight, so I didn't go by the mailboxes."

"Well, show him your dictum, Earl," Tomlin said. "I threw mine away already."

Fox pulled a piece of folded paper out of his shirt pocket. The shirt was green with pink flamingoes on it. He handed Burns the paper.

Burns unfolded it and read it. It was a memo from Miller, reminding every faculty member to have office hours posted on office doors and commanding everyone to have at least one afternoon office hour a day.

"What brought this on?" Burns asked.

"I heard a rumor that one of the board members saw a faculty member downtown having coffee in a cafe at ten in the morning," Tomlin said.

"What's wrong with that?" Burns asked.

"We're supposed to be tied to the office," Tomlin said. He ground out his cigarette butt in the ashtray and lit another. "Wouldn't do to give the public the idea that we aren't working."

"Does the public see us when we're teaching night classes?" Burns asked. "Does the public see us when we take home a stack of term papers to grade at night or on the weekend?"

"The public doesn't care doodly-squat about that," Fox said. "They just don't want us going for coffee at ten o'clock."

"All right, I won't," Burns said. He gave the memo back to Fox.

"And it doesn't look good for the rest of us if you keep finding dead people," Tomlin said. "I'm surprised they haven't gotten around to writing a memo about that."

"They will," Fox predicted. "You hide and watch. They will."

"Probably," Tomlin said. "Aren't you going to smoke today?"

"Damn right I am," Fox said. He got a pack of Alpines from the pocket that had held the memo. "Generic price," he explained as he lit up. "Better-looking package than those Cost Cutters, too."

"Absolutely," Tomlin agreed.

As much as he hated to leave such cheerful companions, Burns wanted to talk to Mary Winsor and Abner Swan. Particularly Swan. When Napier had mentioned sneaky individuals, Swan had popped into Burns's mind at once. Though Swan was outwardly an asskisser from the word go, Burns had always pegged the man as a sneak, just the type to write poison-pen letters.

Some years previously there had been a young chemistry teacher named Bentley who had fallen in love with one of his students. He had begun dating her quite openly. There was nothing wrong with that, neither of them being married to anyone else, but Swan objected. It was too blatant, and if Dick Hayes had once done the same thing, at least he had kept it hidden.

Swan, however, never said anything to the young man. He voiced his objections only to other faculty members he believed might be sympathetic to Bentley and his lover, and Burns knew of the whole thing only because someone had told him.

Burns found out what happened next, though, because Bentley confided in him.

"Somebody's calling me," Bentley said. "At pretty odd hours. Midnight, two-thirty in the morning, like that. It's beginning to get to me."

"What are they calling about?" Burns asked.

They were in Burns's office, a relatively safe spot, but just as Don Elliott always did, Bentley got up and closed the door. "About Sara."

Sara was the student Bentley was dating.

"What about her?"

"They say things like, 'If you don't quit living in sin with that slut, you'll burn in hell.' Things like that."

"Good grief," Burns said. "Are you living in sin?"

"Not as much as I'd like to," Bentley said.

"Did you recognize the voice?"

"No. It's not always the same person. Sometimes it's a woman, and sometimes it's a man. That's all I can tell."

Burns was not a betting man, but he would have given odds that Abner Swan and his pursy-mouthed wife were the culprits. It was just the kind of thing they would do. Disguise their voices a bit, never say very much, and they would never get caught.

The only advice Burns had for Bentley was to change his phone number to an unlisted one, which the young man did, but nothing helped. The phantom callers got the new number somehow and started their campaign of harassment all over again.

Bentley left the school at the end of the semester and no one ever heard from him again. Swan never admitted anything, but he seemed especially pleased with himself for days after Bentley's resignation was announced.

Swan's office door was open when Burns arrived, so Burns walked right in.

Swan sat behind a mahogany desk. He was dressed in a

navy blue suit with a TV blue shirt and dark blue tie. His hair was carefully styled and waved. Burns wouldn't have wanted to pay the man's mousse bill.

The desk was decorated with a life-size sculpture of the Praying Hands, and the walls were hung with enlarged photos that Swan himself had taken while on a tour of the Holy Land many years before. There was a shot of the Wailing Wall, one of the Jordan River, one of the Mount of Olives and several others. Burns had to admit that they weren't bad.

"Good morning, Burns," Swan boomed. "Lovely day, isn't it?"

It was, to tell the truth, sunny and a bit cooler than the day before—a lovely day indeed, but Burns knew that it wouldn't have mattered to Swan if it were hailing iceballs the size of grapefruit. He always said it was a lovely day, just in case God was listening in. Swan didn't like to take any chances.

"I understand that you're working on these terrible crimes for President Miller," Swan said. "An excellent move on the president's part, I must say. You've got a real talent for investigation, Burns."

"You might say that," Burns said, tired already of the man's gushing. "For one thing, I've found out something about you that I didn't know."

Swan looked a bit taken aback. "You've learned something about me?"

"You, and a certain choir director," Burns said.

"My God," Swan said. He got up and walked around Burns, closing the office door. It seemed that being around Burns created a need for privacy in people. "Where did you ever hear such a thing?"

"Around," Burns said. "It's common knowledge. Street knew it, too."

Swan sat back at his desk and buried his head in his hands. Burns didn't say anything. He was going to wait Swan out.

After a few minutes, Swan looked up. His eyes were red, which Burns thought was a neat trick.

"You want to talk about it, Abner?" Burns asked.

"It was more than thirty years ago," Swan said. "I wasn't married at the time."

"How about the choir director?"

"Her husband didn't understand her," Swan said.

Oh brother, Burns thought.

"I was giving her counseling. We met after choir practice on Wednesday evenings. We grew close. One thing led to another. You understand."

Burns understood, all right. Swan probably thought he was telling a story that was unique in human history, whereas it sounded like a thousand stories Burns had heard and read before. He wondered how Swan could admit it and still have the gall to be one of the most self-righteous, holier-than-thou Puritans Burns had ever met.

"I don't understand one thing," Burns said. "I don't understand how Street found out about it."

Swan's face took on a hangdog look. "The man deceived me. He seemed to be genuinely interested in people, and he was a good listener. But all the time he was just gathering material for his books. Even when he was told things in confidence."

"I'd think you'd know better than to tell something like that," Burns said.

"I was young, inexperienced in the ways of the world. How was I to know he would threaten to expose me? So many years had passed. And then you—" Swan pointed his finger accusingly—"you had to bring the man to our campus, long after he should have been forgotten."

"It wasn't my idea," Burns said.

"Of course it was. Who else but an English teacher would want a man like that to come here and fill the ears of anyone who would listen with salacious filth?"

"What?"

"Oh, you don't have to look at me that way. I know the kind of works you discuss in your classes, things by atheists like Shelley and libertines like Byron. Stories by Catholics, like that O'Connor woman, and stories that use the worst kind of language. What must our students think? What will they become?"

"I don't know," Burns said. "Do you think they might fool around with their choir directors?"

Swan looked at Burns with pity. "Oh, yes, that's always the way. Proclaim me a sinner, though my sins are long forgiven, unlike yours. You are the one who brought that man here, and therefore you're responsible for his death."

"I didn't kill him," Burns pointed out. "I thought maybe you did."

Swan stood up. "How dare you suggest such a thing! I tried to keep him away! I—"

He stopped, knowing he had said too much.

"That's all right," Burns said. "I had you figured for the letter to the newspaper. There wasn't a word of truth in it, was there?"

Swan slumped into his chair. "No, it wasn't true. I made it up. How could you have known I sent it?"

"A man's character is his fate," Burns said.

"That's not Biblical," Swan said.

"No, but it has a certain ring to it. Look, Abner, I don't care now if you wrote Duncan that letter. I just want to find out who killed him and Street."

"I didn't do that," Swan said. There was something in his tone that indicated he wasn't terribly sorry that Street, anyhow, was dead.

"I didn't think you did," Burns said. "People who resort to writing letters and making phone calls usually don't have the guts to kill anyone or do anything else that requires a face-to-face meeting."

"What do you mean about phone calls?" Swan asked.

"Never mind." Burns got up to leave, but when he got to the door he turned back. "Speaking of phone calls, did Street call you after that dinner the other night?"

"Yes," Swan admitted. "But I wouldn't talk to him. I hung up on him. I didn't have to listen to his abuse if he didn't have the nerve to face me."

Burns was disgusted. "It figures," he said. He went out into the hall.

"I'll pray for you, Burns," Swan called after him.

"Don't bother," Burns said.

Burns stopped by the library after leaving Swan's office. Elaine was sitting at her desk, looking at her trophies.

"Did you get things organized in the stacks?" Burns asked.

Elaine smiled. She had a wide, generous mouth. "Yes, finally. It wasn't too bad, really. How's the nose?"

Burns reached up and touched it. "Fine. I hardly notice it now." In fact, it wasn't bothering him at all. His head was still sore where he had banged it on the tractor seat, but he wasn't going to mention that.

"R. M. called me this morning," Elaine said.

"Who's R. M.?" Burns asked.

"Chief Napier," she answered, looking at him as if he were stupid. "He doesn't go by his name, just the initials."

"I see," Burns said. *R. M.?* He didn't like this at all. "What did he want?"

"He just wanted to ask me a few more questions about what happened in the stacks. He thinks he's close to cracking the case."

"Cracking the case?"

"That's police talk. About the attack on you here in the library. Anyway, he said he wanted to come by and talk to me about it some more this afternoon."

"He wants to come by?"

Elaine looked concerned. "Are you sure you're all right? You keep repeating things."

"I'm fine," Burns said, hardly believing what was going on. What a rat Napier was! He would never have suspected the chief of being a Don Juan. More questions about the incident in the stacks, indeed. The very idea! Burns had "cracked the case" of the library attack last night. All Boss Napier

• 163 •

wanted was to see Elaine again. Burns didn't tell her that, however. He would talk it over with Napier, instead.

"You're certainly quiet," Elaine said.

"I was just thinking about the case," Burns said.

"I'm sure you don't need to worry about it. R. M. is certain he knows who was behind it."

"Did he tell you who that was?"

"No. He said that he might have to keep it a secret, since the perp might be involved in other aspects of the case."

"The perp?"

"You're repeating things again."

"I just wondered if that was more police talk," Burns said.

"Oh. Yes. It means perpetrator, I believe."

"Thanks. Well, I have to go talk to someone." Burns wanted to scream, but he kept himself under control. "Are you still going to the game on Saturday?"

"Sure. I'm looking forward to it."

"Me, too," Burns said, but somehow he wasn't looking forward to it as much as he had been.

Burns passed several people on his way to the warehouse, students and faculty alike, but he merely waved to them and went on. His mind was occupied with thoughts of Elaine and Boss Napier. He wasn't jealous, he told himself, but somehow he wished he hadn't found out that Napier was a real human being who collected toys and painted miniature figures. Thinking of him as a lout made it easier to hate him.

When he reached the warehouse, Burns went inside and looked around. Things looked different with the lights on, and he could see the lawn mower he had fallen on. It was bright red. And he hadn't hit his head on the seat, which was padded. He had probably hit it on the steering wheel or the shift lever.

He went into Fairly's office. Clarice Bond was at her desk.

"C'n he'p ya?"

Burns had talked to Clarice enough to know that she had asked if she could help him. "I'd like to talk to Mr. Fairly."

She looked up at him, the fluorescent lights reflecting off her glasses. "'es' inair."

"He's in there?" Burns asked, gesturing toward the inner office door.

"'s'wat sed."

"That's what you said."

"'s'wat sed."

Burns gave it up and went into the other office. Fairly was at his desk, looking at something that might have been a master plan of the campus.

"Hello, Dr. Burns," he said, laying the plan aside. He had a deep, gravelly voice that seemed somehow to go with his widow's peak. "Having any more trouble with the pigeons?"

"Now that you mention it, no," Burns said. "But haven't you been listening to the radio or reading the papers?"

Fairly looked sheepish. "Yes, I have. I'm really sorry about that. I didn't know any of that would happen. I guess I underestimated the number of pigeons, not to mention the effects of the poison."

"What about shooting them?" Burns said. "Wasn't that awfully dangerous, too?"

"You know about that?"

"I heard you up there. And I saw you and your son coming down from the attic."

"Well, that wasn't really dangerous," Fairly said. "It was just my son's .22 rifle."

"I read once that a .22 bullet can carry for miles."

"That may be true," Fairly said. "But he wasn't using bullets. He was using birdshot. It probably wouldn't even break the windows."

Burns thought about that. It sounded logical.

"It wasn't efficient, though," Fairly went on. "He killed a few, but it was too dark to see well, even with the light we carried up there. So I tried the poison."

"That certainly seems to have worked," Burns said.

"Yep. But we'll have to go back and carry off the carcasses."

Burns was glad that was going to be taken care of. "About the windows, . . ." he said.

"We'll fix those, too. Maybe not put in new glass, but we'll nail some tin over the openings."

That would work better than cardboard, Burns thought. "Is anyone going to tell the city council or the police about whose fault all the dead birds are?"

Fairly seemed embarrassed. "No, I guess not. I mentioned it to Dr. Miller, but he said the school had already had enough bad publicity. Anyway, the worst is over."

Well, maybe no one would find out, Burns thought. "I'd like to ask you a few things about Edward Street," he said, changing the subject.

"A fine man," Fairly said. "I owe a lot to that man."

Burns was stunned. "Do you mind if I sit down?" he said.

"Of course not," Fairly said.

Burns sat in an old chair stuffed with what might have been horsehair and covered with cracking leather. "You liked Street?"

It was Fairly's turn to look surprised. "Didn't everyone? He was a great guy. Got me out of a tough situation. I could've lost my job."

"I heard about that. How did he manage it?"

"President Rogers liked him. He knew Speed was working on a book. Speed told him that if he finished the book, the school would be famous. So Rogers didn't fire him. And Speed was right about the book."

"Speed?"

"That's what he liked for me to call him. He was a track star one time."

"I know," Burns said, still amazed. "And he never asked you for anything, never wanted a favor in return for saving your job?"

"Nope. Not a thing. Like I said. He was a good guy."

Burns shook his head. This was as bad as finding out that Napier collected toys. It appeared that even Street had a human side.

"Did he ever mention his new book to you, the one he was working on?"

"I didn't know anything about any new book," Fairly said. "He called me the other night, just to say hello and talk about the old times for a minute. He was quite a guy."

For a minute, Burns thought that Fairly might be lying, but the man was so obviously sincere in his admiration for Street that Burns was convinced of his truthfulness.

"So he really did get you out of a jam?"

"He really did." Fairly looked around his office. "Believe me, Dr. Burns, I learned my lesson. I never took another hit. I don't even drink. Street saved my ass, and I never forgot it. You know what my kid's name is, the one with the .22?"

"No," Burns said. "What is it?"

Fairly smiled. "Edward," he said.

Burns left the warehouse more puzzled than before. He had talked to a lot of people, all of whom had at least a slight motive for killing Edward Street, with the exception of Fairly, who really seemed to believe that Street was a wonderful fellow.

Yet Burns couldn't seem to find any convincing evidence that the other people he had talked to were guilty of murder. How did the police do it? he wondered. They gathered evidence, of course, which consisted of a lot more than talking to people, but how did they know what evidence to gather?

He had confronted just about everyone except for Mary Winsor and Miss Darling. He would try Mary again, and then Miss Darling, if she was still on campus. He didn't put much hope in catching either one of them out, but Mary had not told him about her affair. Obviously she had something to hide.

One of the people he had talked to must have committed

the murder. That much he was sure of. All he had to do was decide which one it was, then call in Napier.

Napier. That snake! Sam Smooth, that was what he was, though you would never guess it to look at him. Burns wanted to talk to Napier, all right, and he had more to talk about than murder. What right did he have to horn in on Elaine, the first eligible woman to show up at HGC in what seemed like forever? Just thinking about it made Burns angry.

But how could he confront the chief of police? After all, Napier probably thought he had just as much right to chat up an eligible female as Burns did. It wasn't easy being a bachelor in Pecan City, as Burns well knew.

At any rate, facing up to Napier would have to wait. Burns had to talk to Mary Winsor first. Maybe he would solve the murder, and then Napier would be too busy following up on the investigation to bother Elaine.

Burns fervently hoped so.

·17·

Burns thought he was doing pretty well so far, all things considered. He had found out who sent the letter to Duncan, and he had found out who had stolen the books from the library. He also knew who had broken his nose and how the library books had gotten defaced.

That was all to the good. But he still had no idea who had killed Street. And he had been shot at, besides getting his nose broken. He couldn't recall that Philip Marlowe ever got a broken nose.

Mary Winsor was reading a student-written article when Burns walked in her office. "Why doesn't anyone use apostrophes any more?" she asked him.

"I don't know," Burns answered. "For that matter, why doesn't anyone put a comma after the name of a state when the name of the town is used?"

"Maybe it doesn't matter," Mary said, laying the paper aside. "Have you found out anything more about Edward?"

"A little," Burns said. "You knew him pretty well, didn't you?"

Mary looked at him sharply. "Innuendo doesn't become you, Carl."

"I apologize. I didn't know how to bring it up."

"That's all right. I really shouldn't be so snappish. It's just that I ran out of gas on the way to school today and had to walk several blocks carrying a gas can. The gas gauge in my car doesn't work, you know."

"No, I didn't know," he said, though he certainly was not surprised. "Ah, do you mind if we talk about Street instead of your car?"

"I'm sorry. I wasn't changing the subject deliberately. No. I don't mind if we talk about Edward. What did you want to know."

"About . . . well, about . . . ." Burns stopped. He didn't know how to put it. Obviously he wasn't as tough as he thought he was.

"You've probably heard that old rumor about my having had an affair with him. Isn't that it? You don't have to be afraid of saying it."

"That's it, then," Burns said.

"You shouldn't let things like that bother you so much, Carl. Besides, there's no truth in the rumor. Well, maybe a little."

"What do you mean?"

"You know what this place is like as well as anyone. Every day there's a new rumor about something or someone. It's a small community, and we don't have much to talk about, so we talk about each other."

That much was certainly true, Burns knew. He was beginning to see a pattern here, like one of his lists. Dick Hayes had denied everything, blaming Street's story on rumor and misinterpretation of facts. Swan had not denied anything, but the offense Hayes mentioned had occurred before Swan had ever come to work at HGC and the rumor had never affected him or his work at the college. And now Mary was telling Burns that the story about her and Street had been exaggerated.

"There was nothing to that story about Hayes killing his wife, either," Burns said.

"I never really thought there was. I shouldn't have mentioned it."

"Don't worry. He's the one who mentioned you and Street. Why didn't you bring it up, by the way?"

"I really wasn't trying to hide anything. I just didn't think it was important. I can see why you might think it would be, though."

"Did Street call you after the dinner to remind you of that old rumor?"

Mary nodded. "Yes, he did. I told him that he should be ashamed of himself, but that he could put whatever he wanted in his new book. No one would ever believe that I had an affair with him."

"But you did say there was a little bit of truth in the story," Burns reminded her. "How much is a little?"

"Not much. Edward was young, but he was already arrogant, and he liked to talk about himself. The funny thing was that he never really trusted his own judgment about his writing. Because I'd written a few stories that were printed in the big-city papers, he asked me to look over some of the early drafts of *Dying Voices*."

"And did you?"

"Yes. But he didn't want anyone to know he was asking for my help. We used to meet here in this very office in the late afternoons. Someone saw him leaving one day, and that was all it took. It was all over campus by morning."

"That's all there is to it?"

"You've heard of Caesar's wife?"

"Yes," Burns said.

"As faculty members at HGC, we, too, had to be above suspicion. In those days, girls going to gym class had to wear raincoats over their gym shorts. Men were not allowed to wear shorts on campus. PDA was forbidden on campus. In other words, President Rogers ran a tight ship."

"Or seemed to," Burns said, thinking about Hayes and Fairly. "What's PDA?"

"'Public displays of affection.' You could be 'campused' if you got too many marks against you for PDA."

"What does that mean?"

"Campused? It means you were restricted to the dorm."

"That was before my time here, thank goodness," Burns said. "It's too bad Rogers didn't avoid private displays of his own."

Mary knew what Burns meant. "Yes, it is too bad. Anyway, he called me into his office and gave me quite a reading out. I convinced him that nothing was going on, though." She looked at Burns. "I suppose the story's improved over the years."

"I didn't get the improved version," Burns said. "Anyway, I don't guess it would be worth killing anyone for."

"No. I was rather flattered, actually. I told Edward that when he called."

"What did he say?" Burns asked.

"He seemed disappointed. I think he was just trying to create a disturbance. He always did enjoy being the center of attention."

Burns thought she was probably right. He had not known Street for very long, but he seemed the kind of man who loved a disturbance. He had certainly gone out of his way to create one at the dinner, and the letters he had sent were another effort in the same direction. Burns wondered if the man were so insecure in his fame that he felt it necessary to assure himself that it existed by belittling those who had not achieved it for themselves. Maybe he felt that he had become a success only through good luck and constantly had to prove to himself that he was really where he was. Somehow, Burns didn't envy him any longer.

"In other words, you think he was just a lot of hot air?"

"That's right," Mary said. "I can't imagine why anyone would want to kill him for that."

For the life of him, Burns couldn't imagine why, either.

There was a new note from Rose taped to the side door of Main:

PLeAse!
Do Not !!
ThRow DeAD BiRDs!!
iN TRAsh!!!
MaID RoSe

Burns wondered who would have tried disposing of dead pigeons like that. Probably the Phantom. Burns trudged up the stairs to the small classroom he was using as his office.

Melinda Land was waiting for him when he got there. She was sitting in one of the desks on the front row, and her legs were crossed. Burns had not noticed her legs before, probably because he had never seen her wearing such a short skirt.

They were very nice legs.

"You've certainly been busy this afternoon," she pouted at him. She did a very nice pout, too. It took a certain kind of woman to get away with looking like that, but she could do it.

"Have you been looking for me?" he asked.

"It's more like I've been following you," she said, uncrossing her legs.

Burns noticed then that she was holding a notebook and a pen. "Have you been interviewing people?"

"Yes," she said. "But they aren't proving extremely cooperative. Everyone keeps saying that Edward Street had written a book about Hartley Gorman College. They won't tell me what's in it, though, and they all insist that everything he said in it, whatever it was he said, was untrue."

"It's beginning to look that way," Burns said. "Or at least extremely exaggerated. Street was that kind of man."

"You mean there's nothing worth telling about this place?"

"I wouldn't say that," Burns told her, thinking over some of his own experiences. "It's just that if you told the truth, it wouldn't be very sensational, and no one would believe it."

She clicked the tip of her ball-point pen against her white, even teeth. "I think you're wrong. People will believe anything, especially if it involves a famous writer."

"You may be right," Burns said. "Have you considered the possibility that there might not even be a book?"

"What?" She dropped the pen and covered her confusion by bending to retrieve it.

"That's right," Burns said. "One theory is that Street didn't even have a manuscript." He didn't mention whose theory it was. "It's possible that Street just told people that he'd written a book to see if he could get a rise from them, to make them feel insecure while making himself feel superior."

"You've got to be kidding me," Melinda said. "Why would anyone kill him if he didn't really write the book?"

"That's a good question," Burns said. "But I've got a better one. If he wrote it, where is it?"

Melinda didn't say anything for a minute. She just stared at the stain on Burns's ceiling. "Maybe the killer took it," she said at last.

"You may be right," Burns said. He hadn't really thought about that before. "But if the killer found the manuscript, why did he kill Duncan?"

"You think Duncan had it?" Melinda's eyes lighted.

"No. I think he was looking for it in here when he was killed."

"I knew it!" Melinda said, leaning forward in the chair. Her tongue flicked out and licked her lips. "You have it, don't you?"

It had been a while since Burns had been able to get a woman so excited. He hated to disappoint her.

"No," he said. "I don't have it. Duncan may have thought I did, since I was the one who found Street's body."

"I know you don't have it here at school." She sounded very sure. "But you have it at home, don't you?"

"No, it's not there, either. I really don't have it. I almost wish I did."

Melinda leaned back and some of the intensity went out of her gaze. "So do I," she said. "It could mean a lot to me."

Burns remembered what she had said about publishing. He was glad once more that he wasn't at a school that demanded the production of articles every year. No matter how many arguments he heard about how English teachers should also be writers, he was not convinced that the world needed any more articles on Faulkner and Hemingway. How many times need the works of one man be reinterpreted, anyway? Too many articles began with what a friend of his had once called "the academic simper": "Certainly Professor _____'s reading of 'A Rose for Emily' seems basically sound; however, . . ." Ah, those wonderful howevers. And since the Deconstructionists had come along, Burns was beginning to wonder if criticism had any value at all.

"Are you still here?" Melinda said.

"What? Oh. Sorry. Just woolgathering. I know how much finding that manuscript could mean to you. Promotion, tenure, all those good things."

"Oh, well," she said. "Even if you don't find it, I think I'm getting together enough material here for a really interesting personality piece on Edward Street. It might not make *PMLA*, but *People* probably pays a lot better."

"*People* wouldn't do you as much good with the tenure committee as *Proceedings of the Modern Language Association*, though," Burns said.

"True," she admitted. "You are *looking* for the manuscript, aren't you?"

"Only incidentally," Burns said. "I'm more interested in finding out who killed Street. That's sort of what I have to do instead of writing an article."

She put on a pouty face again. "Does that mean you'll be too busy to see me tonight?"

"Ah, . . . uh, no. No, it doesn't mean that. Of course I can see you, if you want me to."

"Good. Could we have dinner again, maybe a little of that wine? I feel the need to let my hair down, have a good time."

The image of that red hair being let down appealed to Burns more than he could say. "Ah, . . . great. Great. Shall I meet you in the club again?"

"No," she said, rising from the chair. "Why don't you come by my room first? We'll have a drink and see what develops."

"Ah, . . ." Burns couldn't seem to quit stammering. He hated himself for it. "That sounds good. Is seven all right?" He would have suggested six, or even five-thirty, but he didn't want to seem too eager.

"That sounds fine. I'll be waiting." She left the classroom, and Burns found himself following her gently swaying behind with his eyes. Life was certainly getting interesting.

"Just a minute," he called out before she got out the door.

She turned. "Yes?"

"What do you think of Boss Napier?"

"Is that the chief of police?"

"Yes," Burns said. "That's him."

"He seems a little crude and insensitive, don't you think?" she said. "Not my type at all. I prefer more intellectual men. Why?"

"Ah, . . . nothing," he said. "Just wondering."

"See you this evening, then," she said.

He watched until she had turned the corner at the end of the hall. She certainly appeared to be a better judge of character than Elaine Tanner. He was glad of that, at least.

After Melinda was gone, Burns went downstairs and to the cafeteria. It was crowded and noisy, as usual, so he got in the sandwich line and left with a pimento cheese on whole wheat. He went back to Main, bought a Mr. Pibb, and climbed up to the third-floor classroom to work on the assignments for the rest of the week.

Having left the Puritans behind in his American literature survey class, Burns was now mired in the "Age of Reason and Revolution," as the textbook called it. He would spend another day on Benjamin Franklin's *Autobiography,* and then move on to the Romantics, an altogether more interesting and appealing group, and one of the highlights of the semester for Burns, if not for the students. Somehow they never quite seemed to share his enthusiasm for James Fenimore Cooper, or even Hawthorne for that matter. Poe was a little better, but things went seriously downhill with Thoreau and Emerson.

And today even Burns was having trouble concentrating on his text. Reading about Franklin's plans for achieving moral perfection usually appealed to Burns, primarily because of Franklin's methodical, list-making approach. But even the account of how Franklin came to add "humility" to his list of virtues could not hold Burns's attention.

Maybe it was because Burns had not yet talked to Miss Darling. He knew that he should have done it already, so he gulped the rest of the sandwich, swallowed the Mr. Pibb, and went to her office.

She was there, grading papers in her meticulous spidery handwriting, the red marks somehow not nearly as insulting as they were when Burns made the same kind of corrections.

He knocked on the doorframe.

Miss Darling looked up, her porcelain-doll face quizzical above the frilly blouse that should have been worn by a much younger woman.

"Oh, it's you, Dr. Burns. Can I help you?"

"I wanted to talk to you about Edward Street if you have a couple of minutes," Burns said.

"Of course. The poor man."

"You knew him when he was here, didn't you?"

Miss Darling nodded, her tight, dyed curls bobbing. "Oh

yes. Yes, indeed. He was such an enthusiastic young man when he first arrived here. I always thought that he would be a success."

"He never pried into your . . . your personal life?"

"Why do you ask that?" Miss Darling's small mouth curved into a grimace of distaste.

"It seems to have been a habit of his," Burns said.

"And a thoroughly unpleasant habit it was, too," Miss Darling said. "But of course you know that. It's not one of the things about him that I like to think about."

"I can see why. But did he ever practice that habit with you?"

Miss Darling looked down at her papers. "He tried," she said.

Now they were getting somewhere. "What did he do, exactly?"

Miss Darling did not look up. "He spied on me."

"He *what?*" Burns could not imagine anyone spying on Miss Darling, for any reason. "Why?"

"It's a judgment on me," Miss Darling said. "Now all the pigeons are dying, and it's a judgment on me."

"The pigeons?"

"Yes. I killed a bird, and now the pigeons are dying."

Burns wasn't sure he was getting the gist of the conversation. He thought about Miss Darling trying to check her gradebook into the library.

"You think the pigeons are dying because you killed one?" he said.

"Of course not. It's because I killed that bird, and Edward Street saw me. Now Edward is dead, and the pigeons are dying."

Now Burns was sure. He wasn't getting it. "Why don't you start at the beginning and tell me the whole story," he said.

"It started with the bird that I killed," she said.

"I'm not too clear about the bird," Burns told her.

"It was a mockingbird, you see. It's a sin to kill a mockingbird. It's also a crime. The mockingbird is our state bird, after all."

"You killed a mockingbird. And Street saw you."

"That's what I said."

Not exactly, Burns thought. Then he said, "How did you kill the bird?"

"It was entirely an accident, I assure you."

"I'm sure it was. How did it happen?"

"You know how the windows sometimes get opened when the air conditioner doesn't seem to be working and birds get in the building?"

"Yes. It happens all the time."

"Well, when Edward was here, the building wasn't even air conditioned. So the windows were open all the time. Birds came swooping around the classrooms on a regular basis."

"Must have been distracting," Burns said.

"It was. But the mockingbird got in one afternoon when there was no one but me around, or so I thought. I got a broom out of the ladies' room and tried to shoo it out the window, but I swung too hard. I caught the bird up against the wall and slapped it with the broom. That's how I killed it."

"What about Street?"

"Oh, it turned out that he was here all the time. Standing and watching me and laughing. I was concentrating on the bird and didn't even hear him until it was dead. I picked it up off the floor—it was just a little lump of feathers, really. It didn't seem to weigh a thing. And there Edward was, laughing."

Street was some kind of guy, Burns thought. He might have taken the rap for Fairly, but that was the only time he'd ever shown a spark of decency.

"He stopped laughing when he saw me looking at him, and he said, 'It's a sin to kill a mockingbird, Miss Darling.' I told him I knew that and that it wasn't nice to sneak around spying on people, either. He told me that he was going to report me to the Texas Parks and Wildlife Commission for killing the state bird if I got smart with him, so I didn't say anything else. I didn't want to go to prison."

"I don't really think they'd send you to prison for killing a bird," Burns said. "Make you pay a small fine, maybe. Maybe not even that."

"Still, it was a terrible thing. I should have been more careful. I've felt bad about it ever since."

"What did you do with the bird?" Burns asked.

"I took it home and buried it. I didn't know what else to do."

Better than putting it in the trash cans, Burns thought. "Did Street ever mention the bird again?"

"Only now and then. But he did call me after he got here for the symposium. He reminded me that he remembered about the bird and that there was no statute of limitations on murder."

"What did you tell him?"

"I told him he could go straight to hell," Miss Darling said, her curls jiggling violently.

"Good for you," Burns said.

"I didn't expect to be taken quite so literally, however," Miss Darling said. "And now the pigeons are dying. It's all some kind of a judgment on me for being so violent."

"No it's not," Burns said. He explained to her about the pigeons. "And I'm sure you didn't have anything to do with Street's death, either."

"If I didn't, then who did?"

"I don't know," Burns said. "But I'm sure trying to find out."

·18·

Burns went next door to talk to Clem, but she was no longer in her office. There really wasn't much more he could find out from her, anyway, since she was reluctant to "gossip." He went on back to the classroom and sat at the desk.

He had thought he was getting somewhere, but he wasn't. Sure, he had talked to a lot of people, and all of them had heard from Street. They admitted that much. But that was all they admitted. As far as they were concerned, Street's book could not have hurt them, since they were not really guilty of anything, or if they were, they weren't guilty of what Street said they had done.

Street could have made them seem guilty in the book easily enough, but that would not have made any difference in the long run. The book—if there was a book, Burns reminded himself—would have been a novel, and you couldn't use a novel to convict anyone. Not in court, at least. A novel, after all, was fiction. The HGC rumor mill had been known, of course, to convict on less. but the people involved in Street's book had survived that rumor mill years before and hung on to their jobs, so what was at stake now?

For Abner Swan, the revelations could be embarrassing

but no more than that. For Dick Hayes, too. But for the others even embarrassment seemed unlikely. No one else had motive enough to kill, not that Burns could see.

There had to be another way to look at it. Napier might have been able to provide the information, but Burns was not about to call that Casanova. He wondered if the police chief had finished his bogus questioning of Elaine yet.

Even as he thought that, Burns realized his hypocrisy. It wasn't as if he and Elaine had any kind of understanding. They had never had a date, for God's sake. They were going to the football game on Saturday, but that was all there was to it. While he himself, on the other hand, was carrying on with Melinda Land in a big way. Well, a big way for him. And he was hoping to carry on in an even bigger way later. So why was he bothered by Elaine's apparent approval of Boss Napier?

He couldn't answer the question, and he turned his thoughts back to the murder. Or the murders, because Duncan had been killed, too. He hadn't really paid enough attention to the killing of Duncan, hadn't even asked anyone about it. If he were a real detective, he wouldn't have let everyone off so easily. He would have asked whether Duncan had questioned them, whether they knew what he was up to, whether they had seen him in the building—all kinds of things like that.

He was not as good at this as Miller thought he was. Tomorrow, he would tell Miller that he couldn't find the killer and that the police would have to do the job. If they could.

Tonight, he was going to tell Melinda Land the same thing and ask her about job vacancies at her university. Maybe he could start writing articles. "Avatar and Archetype: Symbol and Image in *The Heart of Darkness*." Something like that, something that had a colon in it. You had to have the colon.

Writing an article! Jesus Christ! Burns suddenly sat straight up, shooting upright so abruptly that he banged his knee on the underside of the desk. When his knee stopped throbbing, he thought some more, and the more he thought, the more convinced he became that he might be onto something.

After a while he got up. He needed to use a telephone, but his own office was still under police seal, not that there was any reason for it to be. So far as he could see, no one had been there since the morning of the murder.

He thought briefly of calling Napier first, filling him in on everything, and letting him take it from there; but he decided against it. Napier was probably still in the library anyway, and even if he wasn't, Burns didn't have anything solid to go on. Napier would probably just laugh at him. Burns decided he could call the police later.

He went around to the other wing of the floor, where Larry and the Darryls had their offices. Bunni was sitting at the desk in the hallway, reading a history text.

She looked up when Burns came in. "Hi," she said. "Everyone's gone except for me."

"I didn't want to see anyone," Burns told her. "I just wanted to use the telephone."

"Oh. Do you want me to leave?"

"As a matter of fact, that might be a good idea, Bunni. Why don't you go downstairs and get something to drink?"

"I don't have any change," Bunni said.

"I do," Burns said, reaching into his pocket and bringing out two quarters. "Have one on me."

Bunni got up and took the coins. "Thanks Dr. Burns. I think I'll get a Diet Coke."

"Good choice. And then why don't you go on back to the dorm, Bunni. You've put in enough hours for today."

"But it's only two-thirty," Bunni protested.

"That's all right. You can claim the hours on your worksheet. It's not your fault that I'm asking you to leave. I'll take care of it."

"Well . . . ," she said. "If you're sure."

"I'm sure. Give George my love. Tell him I'll be at the game Saturday."

"We're going to win this week," Bunni said, gathering up

her books and hugging them to her ample chest. "It'll be a good game."

Burns doubted it. "I'm sure it will. Now run on down and get that Diet Coke."

"See you tomorrow," Bunni said as she left.

Burns was already punching the "O" to get the campus operator.

Burns parked his Plymouth outside the door of Melinda's room. There were plenty of parking spots at the Holiday Inn in the middle of the week. Pecan City was not exactly a tourist mecca, but the motels did tend to fill up on the weekends, usually with traveling salesmen.

He got out of the car feeling a little weak in the knees and tapped on the door of Melinda's room. He'd thought he might do a jaunty "shave and a haircut," but his hand was shaking and he succeeded only in sounding like a woodpecker with some sort of nervous disorder.

Melinda answered his knock on the door and stood aside to let him in. The room looked disconcertingly like the one in which Street had been killed, but Burns did not dwell on that likeness for long. He was distracted by Melinda Land's state of dress.

Melinda was wearing a translucent white negligee. She turned slowly, like a model. Her hair was loose and covered her shoulders. She really had let it down. "Do you like it?"

Burns's throat was dry. He wasn't sure whether she meant the hair or the way her figure was revealed by the negligee, but either way the answer was the same. "Ah, yes . . . very much," he croaked.

The top of the negligee was cut quite low and exposed a generous portion of Melinda's breasts. While she did not have freckles on her face, as many redheads did, there was a light dusting of them across the white mounds that bulged over the top of the negligee. Burns found them fascinating. Both the freckles and the mounds.

And her legs were even better than he had thought that

afternoon. Of course, he was seeing a lot more of them now, since the negligee kept coming open in front.

"Why don't we have a drink?" Melinda said. She turned to the bedside table, where there was a bottle of wine and two motel glasses wrapped in plastic.

"Ah, . . . fine," Burns said. He was sweating, though the room's air conditioner was working well.

Melinda tore the plastic from the glasses. The crackling noise was the loudest thing in the room, with the possible exception of the pounding of the pulse in Burns's temples.

Melinda poured the wine into the glasses and handed one to Burns. "To a good time," she said, raising her own glass.

Burns raised his glass as well. "To a good time," he rasped.

Melinda sat on the edge of the bed and crossed her legs. The negligee slipped away from them and gave Burns an even better look, practically up to her thighs. She sipped the wine and looked up at Burns over the edge of the glass.

"Why don't you get comfortable?" she said. "Sit down here by me and enjoy yourself." She patted the bed beside her.

Burns walked over to one of the room's chairs, his knees threatening to give way at any moment. The sexual revolution had been a long time ago, as far as he was concerned, and he had missed most of it anyway. He didn't watch much daytime TV, either, so he was quite unused to scenes like this.

He took a drink of the wine, but it didn't do much for the dryness in his throat.

"So," Melinda said. "Have you found the book yet?"

"No," Burns said, feeling calmer now that he was about as far from Melinda as he could get in the small room. "I don't really believe there is one."

She waggled a finger at him. "Now don't start that again. I'm sure there's a book."

"The fact that Street told you there was a book when you went to his room doesn't really mean that one exists," Burns said.

"Of course it does. Why would he lie?"

"Lots of reasons. Maybe he just wanted to impress you. A pretty young professor like you might be impressed enough to slip into a negligee for a *real* writer, someone who wasn't a has-been."

Melinda put her glass down on the bedside table. It was suddenly very quiet in the room. Burns's pulse was no longer pounding, and he could hear the hum of the air conditioner.

"You tricked me, didn't you?" Melinda said.

"I guess you could say that," Burns told her. "I already had a pretty good idea you'd been to his room. I was hoping you'd confirm it, though."

"How did you know?"

"Something you said this afternoon when we were talking about the manuscript. You said you knew I didn't have it there at the school. How could you know that if you hadn't searched my office?"

Melinda shook her head angrily. "I knew the instant I said the manuscript wasn't there that I was in trouble. But then you didn't mention it again and I thought maybe you didn't notice."

"I didn't, not then. I was thinking of something else. But it came back to me. You also mentioned how much the manuscript would mean to you. So I called your department chair."

"You didn't!"

"I did," Burns admitted. "She told me a couple of things you forgot to mention about your situation there. Asked me if you had applied for a job, actually. She said that you were a good teacher, but a bit lazy about research and publishing. That you might do better at a small school where publication wasn't so important."

"That bitch. Anyway, I told you that I needed to get an article published."

"True. But you didn't say that you hadn't published anything in two years, that you were up for tenure this year, and that if you didn't at least have a credible acceptance, a highly credible acceptance, you were going to lose your job. 'Three years, up or out,' is the way your chair put it, I believe."

Melinda picked up her glass and drank the wine straight

down, all of it. "You don't know what it's like," she said when the glass was drained. "You don't understand the kind of pressure that there is in a place like that."

"No, I guess not," Burns admitted. "I'm just surprised that you were ever hired."

"Oh, I had published before. In the good periodicals. Enough articles to land the job, anyway. And I had good recommendations. I'm really not a bad teacher."

"I'm sure you're not." She was a damned good actress, at any rate.

"But lately I just haven't had any luck. The publications in the field are so snowed under that even if you get accepted it might take years for the article to see print. And the editorial boards have gotten incredibly picky. If you aren't Harold Bloom, you don't have a chance."

"So you thought a seminar on Edward Street at some little backwater college like Hartley Gorman couldn't afford to be picky, and you sent them a paper. Well, it worked."

"It wasn't enough for the department, though. They wanted something big—*Twentieth Century Fiction,* at least. I was going to submit the paper there after I read it."

"You called Street after the dinner and told him about the paper you'd written. He probably invited you over. Someone at the dinner told you about the manuscript of a new Street novel, and you probably thought you'd hit a gold mine. What I don't understand is why you killed him."

Melinda poured more wine in her glass. "You didn't know him very well, then."

"You admit that you killed him?" Burns was amazed. He hadn't expected it to be so easy.

"It was self-defense," she said. She drank more wine.

"I find that pretty hard to believe," Burns said.

"Well, it was." She pouted at Burns again, but somehow it wasn't nearly as cute as it had been that afternoon. "He was making filthy suggestions to me, telling me the things he'd like to do to me. He tried to rape me. I shot him."

Burns didn't believe her. "He had a whisky bottle in his hand. How could he have been trying to rape you?"

"He tried to feel me," she said. "He put his hands on my breasts. I shoved him away, and he got the bottle. I thought he was going to hit me with it, knock me out. I had to shoot him."

Burns didn't believe a word of it. He said so.

She shrugged. "I really don't care what you believe. It's what a jury will believe that matters."

Burns still didn't think a woman like Melinda would kill a man for touching her breasts. She wasn't dressed like the type.

"You'd better buy a different outfit for the trial," he said, looking significantly at the negligee.

"Count on it," she said.

Burns had a sudden insight. "Street said he didn't read the papers that were submitted, but I'll bet he'd read them after all. And I bet he told you that yours was tripe." Burns had not known Street for long, but he knew what a sweetheart the man had been.

Melinda's face reddened. "He said it was 'bullshit,' to be precise. He said he was going to say so at the seminar."

"No publication, no tenure. Just embarrassment," Burns said. "No wonder you shot him."

Melinda took a deep breath. "I told you. It was self-defense."

"Of course it was. And you just happened to have a pistol."

"I carry it in my purse. You've never been on the University of Houston's University Park campus, have you? There have been any number of rapes and assaults there in the last few years. I bought a pistol for protection."

"You don't teach at that campus," Burns pointed out.

"I taught an extension class there, at night. To earn extra money."

She might just get away with it in front of a jury, Burns thought. She was certainly pretty enough, and a college professor, besides. Even now, knowing what he knew, he was strongly attracted to her. There were a couple of problems, however.

"What about Duncan?" he asked.

"I had to shoot him, too. He tried to attack me."

"You seem to have a powerfully negative effect on men," Burns said.

"It wasn't the same as it was with Street. I was in your office, looking for the manuscript. I thought you'd taken it. It was supposed to be scandalous, and I thought maybe you were trying to save the reputation of your school. Duncan came up there for the same thing and caught me in the office. He threatened to turn me in if I didn't . . . go along with him. He was a terrible man. I refused, and he attacked me. He must have thought I had the manuscript. So you can see I had to kill him."

"How did you get in my office?" Burns said. He was a little hurt that she had ditched him early just to get to his office. For a while there, he'd really thought she liked him.

"I used a credit card. It was easy."

Even the story about Duncan might be believable, but there was one more thing.

"What about me?" Burns said. "Why did you shoot me?"

"You? I didn't shoot you." Melinda finished off her second glass of wine and looked at him with innocent green eyes.

Burns still had taken only one swallow of his own drink. "Yes you did. You followed me to the warehouse and shot me."

"I didn't *intend* to shoot you. You scared me."

"Sure I did. And I didn't have what you wanted, so you just left me lying there. You didn't even bother to call an ambulance."

"I thought you were dead," she said. "Why should I call an ambulance?"

He couldn't believe it. How could she sit there calmly and tell him all that?

"I'm going to have to turn you in, you know," he told her.

"No you're not." Melinda slipped her hand under the pillow, and when she pulled it back out she was holding a small pistol, probably a .32 if Napier was right. Burns himself didn't know anything about guns, but he could see that hers was an automatic and that her finger was on the trigger.

Suddenly things were not as simple as they had been.

"You, ah, you . . . ." he said.

"You shouldn't have come here and tried to rape me," she said. "You really shouldn't have."

She stood up. The pistol was quite steady in her hand, and Burns found himself thinking suddenly of thousands of old paperback books he had seen. The scene before him would have been perfect on any of them: a cheap motel room, the bed slightly rumpled, a half-empty wine bottle on the bed-side table, and in the foreground the scantily-clad redhead leveling a pistol at the poor klutz in the chair.

And he was the poor klutz in the chair. He had come there thinking he was some kind of Sam Spade. He had al-most been able to picture the scene. He would lay it all out, just as Spade had done for Brigid O'Shaughnessy, and she would plead with him, and he would tell her that he was going to have to send her over. Then she would tell him she loved him, and he would laugh and say that when she got out of Goree in twenty years, then she could come and see him. And then he would call Napier, who would take her away, and that would be that.

She wasn't supposed to be standing there holding a gun on him. It wasn't part of the script.

"You might get away telling a jury there were two attacks on you," he said. "They'll never go for the third one."

"They might," she said. "I'm sorry, Carl."

She wasn't nearly as sorry as he was. Maybe he was in some other book, the one where the cops would bust the door down right about now.

Unfortunately, he had still been upset with Napier and had never called him. There weren't going to be any cops, not this time. It was up to him.

He remembered an old *Peanuts* strip that showed Char-lie Brown on third base, deciding to steal home.

"It's hero time!" he yelled, throwing himself out of the chair and rolling forward in an awkward somersault. He heard the pistol go off, though it was surprisingly muffled, and heard something thud into the back of the chair he had just vacated. He also heard something pop in his neck, but he ignored that as he hit Melinda's very nice legs and made a grab at them.

She tumbled on top of him and tried a couple of smashes at his head with the pistol. One of them hit his ear, which felt as if it were on fire. He hadn't known an ear could hurt so much.

He shoved her off and tried to get up.

She was raking his face and gouging at his eyes with the fingernails of one hand, and then she hit his nose.

He forgot all about the ear.

He yelled at the top of his lungs, and then the pistol went off right beside his head. This time, the sound was not muffled at all.

She hit him in the head with the pistol, and he fell to the side. She rolled him over and got on top of him. He felt her weight on his back and realized that he was now face down. The barrel of the pistol ground into the back of his head.

This wasn't going well at all. It was one thing to get your nose broken by a grown man wielding a book; it was quite another to get beaten to a pulp and then shot by a woman wearing a negligee.

He rolled violently to the side, just quickly enough to avoid a bullet in the brain. The pistol went off again, but Melinda's hand was thrown up and to the side as she was tossed off Burns's back. The bullet slapped the wall.

Burns got to his knees and turned to face Melinda, who was bringing the pistol up again. He knew things were going to look bad if she did manage to kill him. She might even get away with her story of the rape, since there was certainly going to be evidence of a struggle.

He slapped at the pistol, deflecting it just as Melinda fired again, into the bed this time. He grabbed her wrist with his right hand and with his left jerked the bedspread from the bed. As Melinda struggled with him to get the pistol in firing position, he tried to throw the bedspread over her.

She fought it with her left hand, swinging wildly to keep the spread from covering her face, but Burns was just lucky enough to get it over her head.

He let go of her wrist and seized the spread with both hands, pulling it around her like a bag. He gathered it and wrapped her up in it as the pistol fired once more into the floor.

There was nothing to tie her with, and Burns did not know what to do. He didn't want to hit her.

Then he wondered why he didn't want to hit her. He was pretty much of a male chauvinist, he supposed, but it was time he liberated himself.

He judged where he thought Melinda's chin might be and hit her as hard as he could. He felt something snap in his hand, but Melinda crumpled to the floor in a satisfactory heap.

Burns sat there panting for a few minutes.

There was someone pounding on the door.

Burns went wearily to open it. Boss Napier stood there looking at him.

"I thought that was your heap outside, Burns. Disturbing the peace now, are you?"

"I didn't know you answered nuisance calls like that," Burns said.

"Only when they come from motels where there's been a murder recently, and only then when gunshots are involved. You look like hell, Burns. Who beat you up?"

"That woman in there," Burns said, pointing to the orange pile on the floor.

·19·

It had been a busy night after that.

Napier told Burns a few things and then made Burns go through everything that had happened. He made Burns tell it three times or more, but he seemed satisfied that Burns was telling the truth, in spite of Melinda's contentions. Melinda's pistol was in her possession, and it was almost certainly the same gun that had killed Duncan and Street.

"Anyway, the ballistics report will be in sooner or later and we'll know for sure," Napier said. "For right now, we got enough to charge her." He gave Burns a hard stare. "You sure you didn't try to rape her?"

"Of course not," Burns said. "I'm a wimp English teacher."

"Right. She beat you up pretty good, didn't she? You better go to the hospital and get yourself checked."

The emergency room wasn't crowded this time, and after getting his hand bandaged—broken knuckle—and his face treated with antiseptic, Burns went home and called President Miller.

"Congratulations, Burns," Miller said after Burns told

him most of the story. "You didn't have to mention the, uh, the unfortunate incident in the library, I take it."

"No," Burns said. "That didn't come up."

"Excellent, Burns, excellent. I'll remember this. You did a fine job."

Burns thought about asking for a day or two off, but he thought better of it. He also thought about asking when, exactly, Miller would remember this, but he thought better of that, too.

"Thank you, sir," he said. Then he hung up.

The next day when the student body had gone for assembly, Burns went down to the History lounge. The Phantom had been there again. Two more letters had been blacked out, and the sign now said

SMOKING
PUBLIC AREA

Burns sat down in one of the rickety chairs to wait for the others to arrive.

Mal Tomlin came in first. He already had a cigarette going. He joined Burns at the table, but he didn't say anything about the sign.

"You have a date with a wampus cat last night?" he asked. "You look worse every time I see you these days."

"Well, you might say that," Burns told him caressing his broken nose with the hand that had a cracked knuckle. "I expect you've heard all about it by now."

"Most of it," Tomlin said. "The version I heard is probably a lot better than what really happened, though."

"Yeah, tell us what really happened," Earl Fox said as he came into the room.

Then he saw the sign and stopped dead. "I'm getting out of here," he said.

"Don't be such a wuss," Tomlin said. "Have a cigarette." He offered his pack of Merits.

"You two are crazy, that's what you are," Fox said. "If President Miller sees that sign, we can kiss our jobs good-bye. 'Smoking pubic area.' Good grief."

"What the hell," Tomlin said. "Name one person who ever made less money by leaving here."

"He's right," Burns said. "And don't you want to hear what really happened?"

"Well, . . ." Fox said.

"Sure you do," Tomlin said, dragging out a chair with his foot. "Sit."

Fox sat, and Burns told them what really happened.

Fox was disappointed. "She didn't have her nighty all ripped off when the cops got there?" he said when Burns was finished.

"No," Burns said. "I told you. She was wrapped up in a bedspread."

"Damn," Fox said. "The way I heard it was better. If you ever put that in a book, I hope you get her naked, at least."

"A book?" Burns said. "Write a book about this place? Do you think I'm crazy?"

"But what about the manuscript?" Elaine said later that day. She was polishing a trophy that said "World's Greatest Mom." Burns hoped she wasn't keeping any secrets from him.

"Napier didn't tell you when he was 'questioning' you?" Burns asked. "He should have known by then."

Elaine put the trophy down, ignoring Burns's tone. "No, he didn't tell me," she said. "Did he tell you?"

As a matter of fact, he had. Napier had gotten a call the previous day from the police who had searched Street's home. They had been told later that he also kept an office, where he did most of his writing. They had searched it, and they had found the manuscript, more or less as Street had described it. Napier had been wrong about there being no manuscript.

"What do you mean by 'more or less'?" Elaine asked.

"It's sort of the story he described, but it's not nearly

complete. It's also just a rough draft. Probably about fifty pages, no more. Nothing publishable."

"Oh."

"Yes. And the pages were practically yellow with age. He hadn't touched them in years." So maybe Napier had been right, in a way. But Burns wasn't going to admit it.

"It's really sad," Elaine said. "He had talent. He showed that in his two books."

Burns agreed that it was sad, but he had other things on his mind. "What time shall I pick you up on Saturday?" he asked.

"What time does the game start?"

"Eight o'clock."

"Seven-thirty, then. Did you know that R. M. was a football fan?"

"What?" Burns said. "A football fan?"

"Why, yes. When I told him that we were going to the game, he said that he had a ticket himself. He said that he'd look us up and sit by us if there was a vacant seat. Isn't that nice?"

Sam Smooth, Burns thought. *Don Juan. That snake!*

"Yes," he said, forcing a smile. "That's just wonderful."